The intr

It was the sound of the wind that first woke her. Then there was a different sound, a deeper, drawn-out cry of wood pressing against the restraint of nails that bound it. And a distinct click, heard clearly through the howl of the wind rattling past the sign outside.

Claire turned and threw back the covers, shivering as she stepped softly onto the cold wood floor beside the bed and clutched her flannel nightgown to her against the chill in the room.

A rapier-thin beam of light moved in the living room, lashing out from the dark figure of a man. It slashed over and past her.

Claire began to run, faster, heart pounding, but she wasn't moving fast enough. . . .

ABOUT THE AUTHOR

Laura Pender, who is kept very busy by a
permanent job and two young children,
recently moved to the Minneapolis,
Minnesota area. Laura's spouse contributes
heavily to her Intrigues, and in addition to
writing them, Laura has written for *Alfred
Hitchcock's Mystery Magazine*.

Books by Laura Pender

HARLEQUIN INTRIGUE
62–TASTE OF TREASON
70–HIT AND RUN

Traitor's Dispatch

Laura Pender

Harlequin Books

TORONTO • NEW YORK • LONDON
AMSTERDAM • PARIS • SYDNEY • HAMBURG
STOCKHOLM • ATHENS • TOKYO • MILAN

To Linda, whose insight and intelligence
is always more than invaluable,
and to Randy and her fine antique store—
may they never change

Harlequin Intrigue edition published June 1988

ISBN 0-373-22091-X

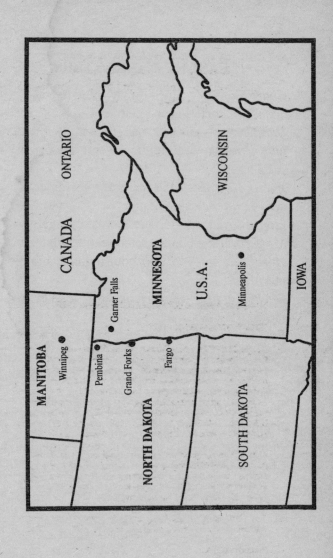

CAST OF CHARACTERS

Claire Hoffner—She'd do anything to track down her uncle's near-killer.

Dan Garner—His past was still a mystery, and his knowledge of unfolding events downright suspicious.

Walter Hoffner—He surprised a customer who arrived *after* closing hours.

Hans Wermager—His credo was revenge.

Moss Hunter—Hans's personal pit-bull terrier.

Harold Jason—He was about to make a fatal mistake.

David Zendler—His friends didn't take betrayal kindly.

Burt Peterson—His dislike for Dan Garner went beyond county lines. . . .

Jimmy Webster—A deputy whose loyalties knew some bounds.

Phillip Hoffner—An innocent, or a key criminal?

Janet Hoffner—She almost served dinner amid a hail of bullets.

Prologue

The man drove through Garner Falls, Minnesota, early Thursday afternoon, December third. Traveling on Highway 82, which served as the town's main street, he paid little attention to the row of storefronts lining the eastern side of the highway except when he passed the antique store between Webster's grocery and the hardware store. Hoffner's Antiques, a hand-carved sign proclaimed from the display window. The man drove slowly as he passed, then accelerated and continued out of town, just another car in an intermittent stream flowing up to Canada twenty-five miles to the north.

Now it was well after sunset and he was back, his dark sedan parked on Willow Street, which paralleled the highway he'd been on earlier. With his car directly across from the antique store, he sat silently behind the wheel, a shadow within shadows. Occasionally the red glow of his cigarette would move up, flare briefly and descend to where he rested his hand on the seat beside him.

The display windows in the two-story buildings along the main street of Garner Falls were all dimly lit, allowing the sheriff or his deputies a clear view of the in-

teriors when they passed through on their nightly
rounds. But Hoffner's window glowed brighter than the
rest. The shadow of someone moving within the store
occasionally slipped over the walls and the displays inside. On the second floor another window glowed, but
that didn't concern him. The man in the car was waiting for the store's occupant to finish his business before he carried out his own.

At nearly midnight the lights dimmed to one bulb,
and a shadow moved over the blinds upstairs in the
proprietor's apartment. When that light, too, was extinguished, the man clamped his cigarette between his
teeth and pulled his car away from the curb, then drove
to the first street crossing to the store. He slowly piloted the car east to the alley running behind the main-
street businesses until he came to the door at the back
of Hoffner's Antiques and stopped.

He waited for a long moment before getting out. Bits
of paper hushed around his legs on the wind when he
carefully closed the door until it clicked into place and
extinguished the dome light. He walked quickly up to
the back door of the shop, slipping on a pair of thin
cotton gloves. He bent over the lock, released it in seconds and stepped in quietly.

Once inside he took a penlight from the pocket of his
dark coat. He was in a windowless storeroom, and the
flashlight beam appeared like a narrow sword of light
in the pitch black. For a moment he played the beam
over the dusty assortment of stacked furniture, then
crushed his cigarette on the floor and strode through to
the main room.

A low-wattage bulb burned in an iron floor lamp by
the desk, casting a tenebrous light through the room.

The merchandise was displayed in random piles scattered haphazardly throughout. But the man seemed to know exactly what he was after. He moved through the cluttered store, past the glass display cases of porcelain figurines and Haviland china to a row of earthenware crocks standing in a disordered stack against one wall. Taking a magnifying glass from his pocket and using the penlight, he knelt on the floor and began a minute examination of the trademark designs. As long as he was quiet he could take time with his work; there wouldn't be anybody dropping by until morning, and he planned to be gone long before then.

Finally the man chose three crocks. He'd given some thought to simply taking all three of them, but where one missing crock might be seen as a miscount, three of them would surely be discovered as theft. He didn't want to put anyone on his trail any faster than necessary. He took all three of the two-gallon crocks to a display case hidden from view of the front window by an old highboy and began to examine them with the flashlight and magnifying glass.

While the man was engaged in his close study, the door leading up to the upstairs apartment opened. Walter Hoffner, the shopkeeper, walked through with a robe thrown over his pajamas.

"Hey!" Walter shouted. "What in the hell are you doing?"

The man dropped his light and magnifying glass and, grabbing one of the stoneware crocks, tried to run to the front door. But he stumbled over a low stool in the dark, almost falling. Walter, galvanized into action, leaped forward and grasped at the rough fabric of the man's dark coat.

"Hold on, buddy! You're not getting away that easy!"

"No?" The man pivoted sideways and swung the heavy pot upward.

A strangled cry burst from Walter's lips as the crockery slammed into the side of his head, cracking along its base. He let go of the intruder and fell heavily against a washstand, trying feebly to stop himself but falling to the floor.

The man hurriedly negotiated his way through the maze of furniture, making sure to replace the two crocks he had removed earlier on the pile near the front. Then he made a headlong flight toward the back door.

Walter Hoffner pushed himself up from the floor, managing to lift himself to his feet and stagger back to the desk. He raised the receiver of the telephone and dialed one number before his knees gave way. He sank heavily on the floor by the desk, the receiver clutched in his hand.

He barely heard the voice of the operator through the hiss surging through his ears, but he managed to answer.

"Help," he said hoarsely. "Help. Police."

His voice trailed off as the receiver clattered to the parquet tiling.

AN HOUR AFTER Walter's call, a telephone rang in room 324 of the North Star Hotel in Winnipeg, Manitoba, one hundred miles north.

The man lying in the bed threw his arm out and snatched the receiver from the phone before it could ring again. "Yeah?"

"Dan, wake up!" The caller spoke excitedly, commanding the attention of the tall dark man who rolled halfheartedly to the edge of the bed and pushed himself up. "There's been a break-in at the store!" he shouted.

"What am I supposed to do about about it at this time of night?" Dan swung his legs out of the bed and stood, raking his fingers back through his sleep-tousled thatch of mahogany-colored hair. An expression of irritation creased his firm, honest features.

"Get down there. With Hoffner hospitalized, we've got to take a more active part in this mess."

"Wait a second." Dan stood rock still beside the bed, moonlight gleaming on the suddenly tensed muscles of his bare arm and broad shoulders as he gripped the receiver tighter. "Walter is in the hospital? What happened?"

"Surprised the burglar and got clobbered for his trouble. There's obviously a third party involved."

"Damn!" Dan sat heavily on the bed. "What condition is he in?" he said.

"I don't know."

"You're a lot of help, Peters. What hospital is he in?"

"In Grand Forks, I think. What's the deal?"

"I'd better get down to see him." Dan reached for the jeans lying on the empty bed next to his.

"Hold on, Danny. You've got to get down to Garner Falls and get a lock on the merchandise."

"I don't have to do a damn thing!" Dan shouted into the receiver, holding the trousers crumpled tightly. "I resigned, remember? I have to find out about Walter."

"You're still working for the Department of Justice and you won't be out until you get a release from Washington, Garner. Not a minute sooner." The voice on the phone was insistent, harshly demanding. "We've started the paperwork, but until it's been processed, you still work for the government. I can always seal your file and let things lay as they are."

"But I turned in my badge already."

"Lack of a badge doesn't change your status. After all, you accepted your present assignment without one."

"That was when we were focusing on Hans Wermager personally. Now the game is wide open, and you can send anyone in."

"No, we can't. The game is far from open, and you're perfect for the job, Danny. You're the only agent with a working knowledge of the people in town. It will take too long to bring another agent up to speed on this thing."

"Just what kind of cover can I use down there?"

"Is it so odd to go back to your own hometown for a visit?"

"But my family hasn't lived there for nearly twelve years."

"Don't give me any more excuses." The man on the phone hardened his voice into an authoritative growl. "We've got to recover the papers fast. Now you get your tail down there and do the work you're paid to do."

"Can you at least find out how Walter Hoffner is and get back to me?" Dan lay back down on the bed in resignation.

"Yes, if it's important."

"You're damn right it's important," Dan said. "I'll get down there tomorrow, but I want to know about Walter first."

He hung up the phone before the other man could make any reply and laid quietly on the bed. After several minutes he stood up and slipped into the pants he'd been holding. Then he took a cigarette from the pack on the bedside table and lit it.

He sat in the chair by the window, smoking and staring out at the winter night. He remained there, unsleeping, as the orange light of dawn brightened on his stoic features.

Chapter One

"He was so pale," Claire Hoffner said. She pressed the slender fingers of her right hand against one temple, combing them back through her dark auburn tresses. A worried look creased the faint line of freckles across the bridge of her petite nose. "I wish the doctor could have been more certain about his condition." She stroked one finger over the silken collar of her light blue blouse, which was wrinkled now from travel, and tried to come to terms with the impossible image of her uncle injured and in the hospital.

Phillip Hoffner sat quietly for a moment studying his cousin's face, saddened by the worry clouding her green eyes. He marveled again at what a fine woman his cousin had grown into—slim and athletic and with a confident cast to her clear oval features. In her cashmere topcoat, worn over gray wool slacks and silk blouse, she looked like a beautiful, prosperous businesswoman. Only a grim look marred the otherwise perfect picture she made. Even now she put forth an aura of vitality that seemed to push back some of the gloom of his thoughts.

"There was no indication of brain damage, so that's a blessing." He spoke with feigned optimism. "I guess it all depends on how strong Dad is. And we both know he's not exactly a ninety-eight pound weakling. He'll wake up any time now." He smiled, but it didn't last. "I wish you would have given us some kind of warning about your travel plans. I could have called and softened the blow somewhat."

It was late afternoon, and they'd just gotten back from United Hospital in Grand Forks, North Dakota, where Walter was rushed by ambulance after the telephone operator traced his phone call and alerted the sheriff. Phillip was going down to see him, and Claire had insisted that he take her with him as soon as she heard the news even though she'd just completed a long trip of her own.

Northwestern Minnesota has a utilitarian kind of beauty, a grandeur achieved through the combination of nature and man's uses of it. As far as the eye can see, broken only by occasional creeks and roads, there is farmland. Large expanses of wheat and barley fields, sugar beets, sunflowers, potatoes and beans, the evidence of the country's bounty lay open around them in a rich landscape.

The flat, almost treeless plains of the Red River Valley of the north seemed to roll on forever as they drove the sixty miles to the hospital. But today the patchwork of fields and farms was devoid of crops, plowed to hard ridges of black dirt and covered with the stubble that remained of harvested crops. The land no longer seemed friendly and inviting, no longer familiar as she and Phillip made the trip down to the hospital and back.

And now they sat in the living room of Walter's apartment trying to cheer each other up. She had been invited to stay in the guest room.

"I didn't really have any plans, nothing in particular to accomplish on my way back from seeing Mom and Dad in Arizona," Claire told him. "So I called Cathy when I landed in Minneapolis, and they invited me to stay a couple of nights."

"Well, it might have been even harder to take over the telephone. I don't know. It's been a lousy couple of days."

"Does Burt have any idea who did it?" she asked, referring to Sheriff Burt Peterson, her father's closest friend and almost as dear to her as her Uncle Walter. He'd been there for every major event of her life, her second anchor in Garner Falls.

"It looks like Dad surprised a burglar in the shop. But I can't think of why a burglar would break into the place. The hardware store would surely have more money on hand, and their locks aren't any better than his was." He spoke with the leaden tone of a man totally mystified by the vagaries of life, a man struggling for an explanation for all that happened and finding none.

"Knowing Walter, I'm sure he ran in to stop the man rather than call for help." Claire couldn't help smiling at the thought of her uncle's stubborn self-reliance. It would never have occurred to him that a man caught in the act of robbing the store might be desperate and too dangerous to deal with alone. When Walter Hoffner saw a problem he dealt with it directly, as he had obviously tried to do with the thief.

"What are you planning to do now?" Phillip asked.

"I haven't thought about it much." Claire smoothed back a chin-length lock of her hair distractedly, her clear green eyes seeming to turn their gaze inward. "I was just going to work in the store for a while. You know, give Uncle Walter the benefit of my experience in the east coast antique trade," she said, letting a smile brighten her oval features. "Beyond that, I had no plans. I suppose I'll keep the place open for him while he's recuperating. Christmas is the peak season."

"That would be good of you." Phillip paused slightly, studying the patterned weave of the couch he was sitting on. "I don't suppose this is the right time to bring it up, but he's leaving you the shop in his will."

"The store? My God, I didn't know that." Claire was genuinely surprised by the news. Her uncle had never spoken of a will, much less leaving anything to her.

"Well, he is. Showed me the papers nearly a year ago."

"He didn't say anything about it any of the times I talked to him."

"I don't suppose he would have. Dad isn't much to talk about death, especially his own. And it isn't my place to talk about his personal affairs. Except that now, well, it just seems like something you should know."

"Let's not talk about it," she said quickly, rubbing one hand over her brow as she watched her cousin look absently across the room. He resembled Walter, having the same lean, angular body, high forehead and cap of thinning brown hair. His sadness and worry had aged him, too. "He's going to make it, Phillip. I have to believe that he'll make it."

Though she spoke positively, the sight of her uncle lying beneath starched linen that afternoon had given rise to doubts that she wasn't able to quell. It chilled her to think of Walter dying, Walter gone from her life.

"Sure. He's tough, and he's no quitter. Still, it's hard to be positive. That's why I brought up that will business. It just seemed like something that had to be said."

"Maybe, but it's not really right, though. That is, I just feel kind of odd being singled out like that. After all, he has you to think of."

"You're the logical choice to get the antique store after all the hours you put in here. I'm not much taken with the antique business. It's all junk to me, and there's sure as hell no money in it around here."

"Maybe, but I still don't feel right about it."

"You know how Dad feels about you. He wants to be sure you'll have something to fall back on, after the divorce and all. Not that he wants you to settle down in this one-horse town and run the place. He said you should ship the inventory back east and sucker premium prices out of the city rubes."

Claire laughed, covering her mouth. "I can hear him saying exactly that," she said.

"Dad's been concerned about you since you became a free woman. You got everything wrapped up with what's his name?"

"His name is Edward," she said quietly. "And yes, I've got everything all wrapped up."

"He paying alimony?"

"No, I've got my own income. I don't need anything from him." Claire looked away, watching the grandfather clock by the kitchen door marking the slow progression of time.

"Should'a got alimony, Claire. You're entitled."

"I got out, and that's all I wanted," she snapped. "Let's drop it."

"Sorry. Touchy subject, I guess." He slid his cup onto the coffee table before him and sat staring down at it.

"A bit tender, perhaps, but no great tragedy. I didn't mean to snap at you." She touched his hand lightly. "I can't drop all my problems at Edward's feet."

"No sweat, it's the price I pay for being nosy. Well, don't worry about having to take care of this joint yet, 'cause old Walt will be running it for a good many years yet."

"Of course he will," Claire agreed. "How are Janet and the kids?" she asked suddenly. "I've been thinking about Walter so much that I haven't even asked yet."

"I understand. We're just fine. Elizabeth has already started talking about boys this last summer, so I suppose I'll have that whole rigamarole to look forward to all too soon." His words didn't sound hopeful, but, when he spoke of his elder child there was loving warmth in his voice.

"It's hard to believe she's already thirteen. And Paul is eleven."

"Just turned. He's quite the little farmer. Better than his dad already. 'Course, that don't take much," he added with a grin.

"The farm is doing well?"

"Almost." He put his cup down on the coffee table before him. "Had a good year, that's true. Seemed like everything I put in the ground came up a bumper crop. And then Wisconsin went dry and drove up the price of beans. Can't be lucky forever, though. I think the bank will have the place yet."

Phillip had always been a bit of an enigma to Claire. A moody man, by turns carefree and dour, she could never be sure what humor she would find him in. But though his darkest thoughts had come more and more to hinge on the balance sheet of his farming operation, she'd never known him to be so open about it. This was a new side to his nature, and she didn't know exactly how to reply to it.

"Come now, it can't be that bad," she said lamely.

"Could be. Probably ain't, but it sure as hell could be for all I've done with the place." He sipped his coffee, then fixed her with his watery blue eyes. "You know how I've been all my life. Everyone knows, but I've only just come to see it. I kept claiming that I was having bad luck with my seed or was making the wrong crop choices, but the fact was that I just wasn't paying attention to business. We were having good years when I started. Prices were up where a careful farmer could actually make a profit. Hell, I made my profit and spent it on new machinery and vacations in Hawaii. I thought the whole point of owning a big farm was to own equipment and live the high life. Trying to live up to the Garners, I guess. So I bought drinks for everyone at the bar and traded for a new car every year till I ended up all but bankrupt last fall. Meanwhile most of the farmers around here plod along with the same tractor they bought when they first got their land and put their money in the bank. They dress like bums, stay home at nights and plan out every facet of their futures. I should be worth twice as much as any of them."

"That's quite a speech. But I don't understand why you're telling me all this."

"I don't know, either. Maybe it's because of the old man. What if he dies while I'm still a failure? I don't know."

"You're hardly a failure."

"No, just mostly." He smiled, wryly. "Don't mind me. Dad's beating has me down, is all."

"Sure, you'll snap out of it. Besides, things are looking up for you."

"They are. I just don't want to admit it, I guess. The bank isn't quite ready to admit it yet, either."

"Do you owe very much?" She asked though she felt it was none of her business, because he seemed to want her to ask. The question of the money he owed was obviously foremost in his mind.

"A lot less than I did, but I've owed it too long in their view."

"I could make you a loan, though I don't suppose it would be much," she offered.

"I wasn't fishing for a loan, Claire." A booming laugh burst out of him, and his eyes twinkled happily. "Though I dare say you've taken in a few bucks off your share of the rental on your old man's farm."

"Well, that, and I sold my interest in my shop."

"Thank you, Claire. It's times like this that remind me why God invented families," he said with a laugh. "But don't worry about me. A year ago, I figured I was headed straight for the poorhouse, but I'll be all right now."

"Then why all this glum talk about money?"

"I've talked my poor wife to the edge of divorce, is why. And I sure as hell couldn't talk to Dad without provoking a lecture on frugality. Now, of course, I couldn't talk to him even if I wanted to. I don't know, I guess I'm sick of talking to the walls about it, and you happen to be handy." He finished his coffee, still smiling.

"Go ahead and talk, then," Claire replied. "I'm glad to have the company."

"Even the company of some gloomy gus?"

"Even that. To tell you the truth, nothing seems right in town and it's got me a bit edgy. I'm half expecting Uncle Walter to come through the door."

"I've got that feeling, too." He looked around slowly, examining the minute cracks running through the plastered walls and ceiling.

"It doesn't seem right that he's not out there somewhere sharing a joke with people on the street." Claire sipped her coffee, watching her cousin. "Even after Uncle Walter comes home, I don't think I'll be able to think of the old hometown in the same way again."

"So you don't think you'll be sticking around."

"No, Garner Falls isn't my home anymore." And for the first time, she knew there was no question about that. With one simple statement she was admitting that her future lay outside the quiet Minnesota town.

"It'll be nice having you around for a while, anyway," he told her.

"I will stay for a while. Walter may need some help when he comes home. And I'd like to help out."

"He'd like that," Phillip told her, then he smiled, saying, "You know, Daniel Garner is in town now."

"Dan Garner?" Claire was momentarily at a loss for words, staring at her cousin blankly as an unwelcome pulse of electricity shot up her spine. Dan Garner, after all these years. "What's he doing here?" she asked slowly.

"I heard that he's looking over some of the family land. Just got into town yesterday. I suppose he'll be around for a visit. Did you two keep in touch at all over the years?"

"No, I haven't seen him since that summer," she said thoughtfully. No, she hadn't counted on seeing Danny on her visit. After hoping in vain for so many years and on so many other visits home that she'd run into him, she didn't know if she could take the sight of him now, not with so much of her life in turmoil. Not with the way they parted so many years before. "Have you ever heard from him?"

"No, not at all. I kind of expected to, though," Phillip said. "We were pretty good friends back in school, and Dad swore by him, of course. Said he was the best worker he ever had on the place besides me. I can't think of anyone else who had much good to say about Dan. Except you, of course. But that was another story." Phillip stood, moving stiffly into his coat. "Jimmy Webster will probably be by tonight. He was asking about where you'd be staying while you're in town."

"Why would he wonder about that?" Claire stood with him.

"He's concerned about you staying here above the shop."

"I would think the shop is the safest place in town now that it's been robbed once," Claire said.

"He thinks the burglar may return if he didn't get what he wanted," Phillip commented. Seeing the flash of worry in her eyes, he quickly amended, "But I think he takes his job too seriously."

A knock cut off the conversation. She hurried through the kitchen to answer the door, which led to the stairway attached to the exterior of the building.

"Claire, you made it!" Burt Peterson threw his arms around Claire as he entered, gathering her up in his tidy scent of cold air and Old Spice cologne. "We didn't know where to reach you and knew you'd be just sick if anything happened to him before you got here. It's good to see you."

"Phillip and I were just at the hospital, Burt," Claire said as they parted. She motioned him into the living room as she closed the door against the wind whistling through the twilight.

Wilson County Sheriff Burt Peterson was a large man, an all-state linebacker who'd managed to keep most of his muscle over the years. One of her father's oldest friends, he'd been her friend, too, earning the title of "uncle."

"Hi, Phil," the big law officer called out. He entered the room and folded his bulk into a chair. "Walter was busy setting up enough card games to last a month, Claire. You know he hadn't won a pinochle game since the last time you were home. I guess this means the tournament is off."

"Don't cancel anything yet, Uncle Burt. On our worst day, Walter and I can take care of anyone in four hands, tops." Claire laughed as she came back into the room and Phillip returned to his chair. Seeing Burt's familiar old hound-dog face brought back the fond memories of bouncing on his knee as a child and drifting off to sleep to the music of her father and Burt in conversation on the front porch on warm summer nights. "Would you like some coffee?"

"Sure, thanks. I was on patrol when Marion Parsons said she'd seen you and Phil in town. I just dropped by to say hello."

"It's good to see you again, Uncle Burt, even under these circumstances. Boy, even after seeing him lying there, I still can't believe it."

"No, and as the law around here, I hate to admit that it caught me flat-footed. You don't generally think of something like this happening in a place like Garner Falls. I just wish I had some idea of what anyone would want in the shop. It just doesn't seem like a very good target for robbery," Burt said. "The shop's been here on Main Street about nineteen years and nobody ever bothered it. Since when did Walter gain the savvy to grab anything valuable for this junk pile?"

"Nobody said the thief had to be smart," Claire said. Burt's good-natured jokes about the shop had been a staple of conversation since Walter took over operation. "He probably thought a one-man operation like that would be more likely to keep cash on hand overnight."

"But he didn't mess with the safe," Burt countered. "There was no sign that anyone had attempted to break it open."

"We'll probably never know who it was, or why he chose the store," Claire said.

"And if he dies, Walt will become another statistic," Burt said bitterly. "A couple of years down the road some egghead will lump his death in with a bunch of others to show how violent crime has risen in rural areas. They'll talk about it on the news for a week or two, and then all those anonymous deaths will go back into the file cabinet until somebody else uses them to show that rural crime has decreased.''

"He's not going to die," Claire stated flatly, feeling the cold prairie wind moving across her optimistic soul.

"No, not hardly," Burt said, quietly. "So, how are your folks?" He took the cup carefully, settling back in the chair. "I heard you were going to fly down to Phoenix for Thanksgiving."

"They're just fine. Retirement agrees with Dad. He's even taken up golf."

"Great, I'll have to brush up on my game and go visit the old duffer." He watched Claire with warm appraisal in his eyes. "What are you going to do now that you're back home where you belong?"

"Run the shop, I guess. I was planning to help Walter with his year-end inventory anyway."

"Sounds like loads of fun, Claire," Phillip said. "And for a really good time, you and I can sit around and complain about the price of wheat."

"Phil is a grand champion at that," Burt said with a snort. "But he just had a damn good year."

"Sure. Forty more like that and I'll be satisfied," Phillip commented.

IT WASN'T UNTIL her visitors left her that she became aware of how alone she felt in her uncle's tidy little apartment. The absence of his hearty voice created palpable gloom. No matter how much logic she applied, she couldn't dispel the dark cloud. He would be all right, she said. He was strong, and the doctor said there was no brain damage. He'd surely come out of the coma any day. But with every positive thought, two negative ones crept into her mind, colored by seeing him lie near death.

Please, not Uncle Walter.

She'd lost Emily, Walter's wife, four years earlier. Walter was left alone in the rambling old farmhouse they'd shared west of town. He'd lost interest in farming after her death and had signed his land over to Phillip, who farmed adjacent acreage, for a nominal payment. For the past three years he'd operated the antique store full-time and lived in the two-bedroom apartment above it. He told Claire he felt closer to Emily, somehow, taking care of her antique business in town, than he did occupying the old house without her.

That was a sentiment Claire could understand now, for Walter's house without Walter in it was empty.

It was Claire's helping her aunt with the antique shop that had prompted her to go into partnership with another woman when she and her husband moved to Vermont. She'd always been close to Uncle Walter, perhaps even closer than she was to her own father. She and her uncle had acted as a team in family games, be it pinochle or billiards, and part of her reason for returning to her hometown now was to reestablish that team by helping him in the shop.

She felt she was at a turning point in her life, poised between everything she had been and everything she would be in the future. Her five-year marriage to Edward Bennett had ended in divorce a year earlier. Now she'd finally broken free of her commitments and left Vermont where he had taken her to establish his law practice. It had been an amicable split, but she'd felt for a long time that she should return to Minnesota, back to her roots, and decide what she wanted to do next. She sold her interest in the store in Montpelier and came home to re-examine her life.

Now, her dear Uncle Walter, her main source of advice, lay in the hospital unconscious and poised on the edge of death, and there was nothing she could do to help but pray.

Junk, her uncle's cross-eyed calico cat, was of no help in cheering her up when he came out of hiding with a suspicious yowl. Walter had taken the cat in from the alley behind the store two years before, overcoming his own distrust of felines to give shelter to the half-frozen wanderer. The cat had quickly found a place for himself in Walter's home, and it was obvious that he resented his adopted owner's absence.

"Here, kitty," Claire called, crouching in the living room. "Remember me?" But if Junk did remember her from her stay in the apartment last Christmas, he wasn't about to show it. He backed under the coffee table and glowered at her. "You'll like me just fine when I feed you," Claire said, pushing back the strands of her chin-length bob as she stood.

Though Phillip had offered her a place in his home, she'd originally accepted Walter's invitation to stay with him and felt it was appropriate that she continue as planned. Someone had to look after the cat, she'd told him, even though it was obvious the cat would accept no one's care but Walter's. Besides, though her cousin lived in a fairly large house, it couldn't exactly be called spacious after adding its two children; she didn't want to wear out her welcome.

Actually it was more for her own piece of mind that she chose to stay in Walter's apartment. She'd come home to think things out after the divorce, and she wanted to do her thinking in what little peace she could find in the empty apartment.

Claire cooked a frozen dinner and ate half of it distractedly, tempting the cat out of hiding with the remaining turkey. Then, feeling at a loss for something to do, she turned on the television and slumped down in the reclining chair.

She couldn't concentrate on the entertainment the TV offered, taking only slight interest in the newsbreak between shows. The newscaster was repeating the story that had dominated the news at Cathy's house in Minneapolis. A collection of Revolutionary War documents on display at the Walker Art Center in Minneapolis had been stolen in a daring burglary. The significance of the documents and the fact that the museum was practically next door to where Cathy and her husband lived in their huge Victorian home made it the primary topic of conversation. So, for the moment it took the newsman to speak his piece, Claire's thoughts managed to leave her uncle.

"There've been no new developments in the investigation of the daring theft at the Walker Art Center," the reporter said. "An FBI spokesman said only that the theft was apparently part of a string of thefts involving Revolutionary War documents carried on by an organized smuggling ring over several years. He said that though they had nothing to report yet, they've been accumulating evidence from several of the robberies and expect a break in the case soon. He described the criminals as hardened, dangerous men reaping huge profits from the sale of historical documents to foreign collectors.

"Among the documents stolen is a recently discovered secret, treasonous dispatch from a Colonial officer, Major James Holloway, to British General Cornwallis detailing the disposition of American forces at the siege of Yorktown in 1781. This one document, had it been delivered, might have prolonged the war for independence at least another year, or perhaps, lost the war entirely. Estimates are that the document could sell abroad for at least one million dollars."

But it was only a sixty-second newsbreak, one small slice of ancient history to interrupt her worries, and it couldn't sway her thoughts for long. So when the doorbell rang, Claire jumped up and hurried to the door, grateful to find Deputy James Webster waiting outside.

"Evening, Claire," he said in a clipped tone as he took off his hat and stepped inside. He wore a tight expression on his broad, honest face, and his sharp blue eyes were pained as he looked at her.

"Hi, Jimmy. Like some coffee?"

"Can't stay. I'm on patrol." He closed the kitchen door behind him, speaking in an official drone belying the long friendship they'd shared since attending high school together. "Hell of a note about Walter, Claire. I wanted to stop by and check on you, and say that if you need anything you should feel free to call on me. It's kind of a lousy welcome back to town, I suppose. But Walt should be up and around soon."

"God, I hope so, Jim. Do you have any ideas about the motive for the attack?"

"No, all we can do is wait and ask Walter when he wakes up."

"Well, I'll certainly help in any way I can, Jim." The topic weighed heavily on her, increasing the knot of worry and frustration growing in her stomach. Wasn't there something hopeful to think about? "How is the family?" she asked. "Did you have a good summer?"

"Can't complain. Did you take care of everything like you said you were going to? Sell your shop and all that?" He smoothed the brim of his uniform cap between his fingers as he stood shifting from one foot to the other.

"I'm all done with it."

"Going to stick around town for a while?"

"A while. Till Walter is healthy, anyway." *If he's healthy,* she thought, darkly.

"I'll see you around, then." He backed toward the door behind him, allowing a small smile to break his official demeanor. "I've got to get back on the street. Now that we've had one burglary, we're patrolling more often. Maybe we can get lucky and catch the guy in the act."

"Good luck, Jim." She placed one hand on his shoulder, the slick fabric of his winter uniform jacket cold beneath her fingers. "I'll see you tomorrow."

"Yeah. Say, Dan Garner is in town," he said.

"So I've heard." Claire spoke noncommittally. "I haven't seen him."

"He stopped in at the station the other day but didn't say much. I wonder what he's been doing all these years."

"I wouldn't know, Jim. I haven't heard from him since he left town."

"We'll have to get together some time," he said, opening the door. "Don't worry about Walter. He'll pull through. Bye now."

If the normally confident James Webster was at such a loss concerning the robbery, then the chances of finding a solution to the mystery were slim indeed.

But somehow events would sort themselves out. Wouldn't they? They had to. Her uncle would recover and life would move back into its well-worn track, because that was the only outcome Claire could stand to contemplate. But even if it did, there was no way to tell if the old hometown would ever seem safe again.

Daniel Garner's visit to town was another event that was sure to affect people's lives. Ever since he left town the summer of his graduation, there'd been unsubstantiated rumors about him and his family. Everyone would be curious to see if any of the rumors were true. Claire most of all, because of the unfinished business between her and Dan.

Garner Falls had been named after his family, which had come from old oil and railroad money. They'd bought thousands of acres of prairie land around the turn of the century and set about farming them with the same determination that had earned them money in their other areas of interest. Dan's father, the third generation of Garners to represent the family in the town that bore their name, had been an aloof and proper man who ran the huge farm with a tight hand. But he'd been the last Garner to maintain hands-on control of the operation, and he had taken the rest of the family back to Minneapolis shortly after Dan left town, leaving the farm in hired hands and the town without a representative of its founding family.

Daniel had been in Phillip's class a year ahead of Claire at Wilson High School in Garner Falls, a wild boy skirting the law and tearing up the countryside in his red Camaro. For one brief year, Claire and Dan had been the magic couple in town. A year older, wiser and filled with reckless confidence, he had captured Claire's imagination even before her heart. In her junior year of school something clicked between them, something that had seemed so real and lasting at the time.

But a couple of weeks after his graduation, he was gone without explanation. The pain of his sudden departure had taken a long time to live through.

Now, sitting with her cup of cold coffee untouched before her on the kitchen table, Claire wondered for the thousandth time why Dan had suddenly disappeared. She had eventually healed, gone on with life, but the question still hung between them and would continue to strain their relationship.

Any annoyance was short-lived with Walter's dilemma foremost in her mind. She felt helpless and didn't like it. Didn't like waiting patiently for his condition to change and didn't like the attitude around her that he'd been in the wrong place at the wrong time. She had to do something, to find out why someone would attack an innocent kind man like her uncle. The answer had to be in the inventory she'd come to help Walter compile. She would have to look, and soon.

DAN WATCHED THE WINDOWS above the shop, lit brilliantly against the night. He had watched Jimmy come and go from his car, and now waited until the lights went out.

There were a lot of things about his life in Garner Falls that he'd forgotten over time, Claire among them. Now all the memories flooded back, the good and bad ones, all the things he'd managed to avoid in the years of constant motion. It was ironic that the job that had kept him safely away from home had finally brought him back there. Further compounding the irony was the fact that he'd finally managed to call it quits. He'd taken steps to sever his ties with the shadowy world of undercover investigation to establish some normalcy in his life. He had come full circle, leaving town on one side of the law and returning on the other.

This time around, would he do everything right?

Chapter Two

"Antique stores are god-awful dismal places." Phillip Hoffner pushed a strand of his thinning hair back from his forehead and squinted around the shop, his eyes adjusting slowly to the unlit interior.

"Dismal?" Claire pulled her heavy wool cardigan closed against the chill air of the store, hugging the brown knit against her. She was wearing snug jeans that showed off her flare of hips. "Where is your sense of history? Don't you have any appreciation of all the artisans who created the implements and works of art for sale in this shop?"

"Artisans hell, it's the people who broke this stuff before Dad got hold of it that deserve all the blame." He picked up the cracked receiver of an old telephone and held it gingerly to his ear. "People actually buy something like this?"

"Not that one," she said with a laugh, joining him at a table heaped with an assortment of household goods. "I remember when your mom bought it from Henry Albertson. I was in high school."

"Mom bought it, huh?" He smiled tightly. "Would it sell in Vermont?"

"Not for much. It's not in very good condition."

"Would any of this stuff sell? Anywhere?" He indicated the pile before them and then moved his hand out to include the other jumbled piles of goods filling the store.

"Well, your dad went a bit overboard with his buying. He wasn't very discerning, I'm afraid."

"More than a bit overboard," Phillip said. He moved a box of framed photographs to the floor and sat on the edge of the table. "The least he could have done was put things in order. The way things are displayed here, you can't find—well, let's face it, things aren't displayed at all. Even a couple of strips of fluorescent lights would help."

"You don't understand antique merchandising." Claire walked around and opened the cash register, absently sorting through the few scraps of paper beneath the change slots. "Fluorescent lights make everything look cold, kind of bluish. And I'm always suspicious of stores that have everything lined up in meticulous order. Of course, the place could use some cleaning. I'll admit that just piling things on a table isn't the best tactic to build sales, but true antique hunters are naturally drawn to places that look pretty much like this one."

"True pack rats." Phillip studied his surroundings slowly. "You're actually going to spend your time hanging around here?"

"Of course. This shop feels so much like home that it might be fun to run it for a while." She closed the cash drawer and opened the drawer in the display case below the register. There was nothing there but the gray inventory book, which she knew from amused experience was not up-to-date, and the large red receipt book with its triple slip pages and the loose sheet of carbon paper. Everything was where it should be, where it had always been.

"Don't let memories tie you to town, Claire, or you'll find that it's ten years later and you're still here working for Dad."

"Is Garner Falls really that bad?" She leaned on the register, resting her chin on her bridged hands. "You've done all right here."

"Sure I have," he said. "I've got a family and over three sections of farmland. But I don't think this place is for you."

"And why not?"

"Well, we're totally lacking in cosmopolitan attractions, for one thing. And there's a drastic lack of single men your age. You'll have to raid the high school for a date."

"Oh, you're hopeless! I'm not going to be in town long enough to worry about getting a date."

"Good for you." He walked back to lean against the counter facing her. "You sure could stay with us until Dad gets back, Claire. We do have a guest room, you know."

"Thank you for offering." She smiled. "But I like staying here. Besides, who'd take care of the cat?"

"Bring the old guy out with you. Really, Claire, it may not be safe staying here."

"It's every bit as safe as it ever was," Claire scoffed. "Even more so now, I'd think. Why would they come back?"

"Why break in the first time?" Phillip raised one eyebrow significantly. "I don't think you should count on anything occurring with any kind of logic."

"No. I appreciate your offer, but this place is special to me. I feel good staying here, even with Walter gone. I'll admit it seemed awful lonely without him last night, but I've gotten over that. Remember when Bertha Mattsen lived upstairs? She helped your mom in the shop the first year it was here. The woman was always baking something; cookies, cakes, bread, everything. The smell of baked goods filled the shop in those days. But Bertha got ill about a year after Emily moved in here. She moved into the nursing home, and these rooms were vacant until your dad moved in."

"But Mom did all of her holiday baking up there while she watched the shop," Phillip said fondly. "I remember coming in here after school and trying to con cookies out of her before Christmas. Seems like every time I did I ended up moving boxes around or dusting something."

"See what I mean? The store is a special place. I can't believe that anything bad could happen to me here. Besides, I want to be here when Walter comes home. He might need someone to take care of him for a while, and you know him, he can't stand to be fussed over. This way I'm already here, and he won't object to having an invited guest here with him."

"You're probably right about that." Phillip frowned slightly, blinking. "If Dad comes home, he'll need help."

"When he comes home," she said, using a hopeful emphasis on her words in an effort to reassure both of them. "Not if, when."

Their conversation was interrupted by the clanking of the cowbell attached to the door.

"I forgot to lock the door," Claire said, walking around the counter toward the front of the shop.

"Sell them as much as they can carry." Phillip forced a smile to his lips as he passed.

A man dressed in a black overcoat entered without a word. He stood examining the items stacked haphazardly in the shop with his gloved hands clasped before him. He appeared to be in his mid-forties, rail thin but broad-shouldered. His wispy brown hair was tinged with gray and combed straight back, brushing the collar of his coat. As she approached him, Claire noted how carefully he appraised the shop while maintaining a casual air. It was a style employed by serious buyers in an effort to compel shopkeepers to drop their prices rather than lose a sale. He was the type she'd come to recognize quite well.

"I'm sorry," she called, hurrying around a large shipping trunk holding a tiffany lamp on its lid. "The store isn't open today."

He turned and stood regarding her for a moment, his dark eyes over a hawk nose as piercing as when they had been appraising the wares on the display. "Not open?" he said. "But your door was open, and there was no sign out front."

"Yes, well the shop would normally be open on Sunday afternoons, but the owner is in the hospital so we're closed." At five foot seven, Claire was nearly the same height as the man and returned his studious gaze in kind, looking straight into his cold eyes.

"I see." The man frowned, his thin lips tightening in annoyance. "That would be Walter Hoffner, wouldn't it? What is wrong with him?"

"There was an attempted robbery, and Walter was injured."

"A robbery?" The man's thin eyebrows rose in surprise. "I wouldn't have expected there to be such activity in so bucolic a setting."

"It isn't common," Claire replied, taken aback somewhat by the man's old-worldly style of speaking. "But I guess there's greed everywhere."

"Yes, there is always greed." He pursed his lips, looking around the shop. "What was stolen?"

"Nothing that we know of. They just broke some of the crockery."

"Crockery?" he said quickly. "I am here for crockery, myself. Stoneware pottery. Was any of that broken?"

"Yes, a Redwing piece, I believe." Claire watched him closely, noting the concern in his eyes.

"Nothing expensive, I hope," he commented, his eyes regaining their casual composure. "May I take a look at what you've got and have you hold the piece for me if I find something I like?"

"I suppose I could do that," she admitted. "But I can't say for sure when I'll be able to open up again."

"I'm interested in Midwestern stoneware and pottery from around the turn of the century. Where would that be?"

"Here, near the door." She led the man toward the disordered shelves of pottery and knickknacks along one wall. "It's all jumbled together, I'm afraid. These ceramic items come from all over, both foreign and domestic, but the larger crockery pieces on the floor are Midwestern. Redwing, mostly."

"Yes, I see." He stepped quickly up to the rough glazed stoneware crocks, stooping slightly to look through the selection. "Are they all authentic?"

"Certainly."

"They do look authentic," he mumbled. "I'm looking for a two-gallon crock for my collection."

"Two-gallon crocks aren't that rare," Claire said. "We have several in the shop, so you should be able to find one easily enough. Finding them with lids, of course, is a different matter."

"I don't need lids." The man lifted one of the clay jars and held it up to examine in the sunlight filtering through the display window. "This is very nice," he said, examining the label, a gleam of appreciation in his eyes. "I collect specifically the Redwing Union Stoneware pieces." He rapped one knuckle lightly on the base of the crock.

Then the man sorted through the selection and examined each of the two-gallon crocks in stock. Nine of them in all were held up to be tapped lightly on the base and discarded until he looked up at her, disappointment stamped on his face. "No others?" he said.

"No, this is all we have, as far as I know."

"Strange, I had thought you would have more in the two-gallon size." He bit the words off as though the selection of crockery had angered him in some way, then smiled thinly. "Well, I don't see the one I want at the moment," he said, standing. "I may be back later, though. In a week or so."

"Good. I hope we can help you." Claire accompanied him to the door.

"Thank you very much. I'm sorry to have disturbed you," he said, stepping out into the cold but sunny afternoon. Then he turned back toward her. "I wonder if you still have any pieces from the—no, you wouldn't know about that, would you. I'll come back at a later date. Good day." His eyes narrowed with piercing appraisal at her, then he turned and crossed the highway to a gray Ford parked at the curb.

"Bye now." Claire locked the door behind him, watching the street for a moment.

As he got in and drove away, she noticed a man rise up behind the wheel of a dark sedan parked several cars away from her visitor. It looked as though the man had been looking for something on the floor of his car, but all he did after sitting up was watch the Ford move down the road.

"See what I mean?" Phillip spoke up from where he'd been standing by the register. "Stores like this attract nuts. If you hang around here, you'll spend your life waiting on spooky men searching the world for the perfect two-gallon crock with a lid. You'd best be sure to hit the trail as soon as Dad can stand to run it himself, Claire."

"That guy wasn't spooky." She turned back toward the lanky farmer contemplatively.

"Sure he was. He had the hollow-eyed stare of some B-movie zombie. Or a true antique lover."

"You're hopeless." Claire pushed up the sleeves of the heavy sweater that was part of her favorite working ensemble of well-worn blue jeans and simple, white cotton blouse. "Now, if you want to hang around here, you'd better be ready to work. I'm going to do a bit of sorting and organizing around here."

"Can't." He smiled. "Janet will have dinner waiting."

"Yes, you'd better get home. But come on back any time when you want to help out."

"Believe me, I'm helping you by leaving," he called out on his way to the door. "Come on out to the farm if you get hungry. If you miss dinner, there's always leftovers."

"Don't think I won't," she answered, smiling as the door closed solidly behind her cousin.

THREE HOURS OF WORK organizing the shop according to type and approximate year of manufacture had barely made a dent in the appearance of the shop. But it was a good start, and Claire went up to the apartment feeling happy about her progress so far. By the time Walter returned, she'd have things sorted out and a complete inventory. If she knew her uncle, he'd be grateful to have it done for him.

Claire brewed a pot of coffee and washed up quickly in the apartment. After a short break, she'd tackle the job of arranging some of the larger pieces.

Walter had done a fine job of fixing up the old apartment since he'd moved in. Emily's cross-stitch pictures adorned the walls of the simple kitchen, and he'd brought many other touches of their farm home with him to town.

One thing he'd added since Claire had been there last was the grandfather clock in the living room. It was a beautiful piece, standing at least seven feet tall, encased in a rosewood cabinet. She could understand his attraction to it but unfortunately the beautiful clock looked terribly out of place standing like a sentry against the living-room wall. It demanded more space, a higher ceiling and a broader sweep of floor before it.

As she sat in the wing chair by the window, the clock announced the hour with a progression of chimes as delicate and pure as church bells heard from far away. No wonder he wanted the clock. Four o'clock.

The fine old grandfather was half an hour fast.

Claire walked over and opened the hood door and moved the hands to correct the time. Then she opened the trunk and adjusted the weights to wind the mechanism. There, another good deed done.

She turned off the coffee maker, rinsed out her cup in the sink and went back down to the shop.

There was a familiar scent in the air as she started down the stairs. Cigarette smoke, fresh and acrid, wafted up from the interior of the shop in a thin vapor. The odor brought her to a halt, one hand pushing back a strand of hair that had escaped the banana clip. She didn't know anyone with business in the shop who smoked. For that matter, there shouldn't have been anyone in the shop at all. She had locked the door after letting out her disappointed customer, and she'd heard it snap shut behind her cousin. She continued down and through the open door into the shop, squinting against the glare of the setting sun to see who was there.

Then a man cleared his throat amid the jumble of furniture and bric-a-brac.

"Is there somebody here?" she called resolutely, walking quickly into the main area of the store. "We're not open."

"I'm sorry, but the door was open." A dark-haired man, slightly over six feet tall, stepped out from behind a warped chiffonier.

Dan Garner stood clad in a worn pea jacket that hung open to reveal a blue work shirt tucked into his jeans. Casual and confident as always, older but not changed, he stood regarding her with quiet brown eyes and a tentative smile on his full lips. It lit the square-cut features of his face even as the sunlight filtering into the shop seemed to glitter on his curly brown hair. He was holding a cigarette in his left hand, and his right hand hooked a thumb in his pants pocket.

"I heard you were in town," she said, approaching him.

"Hello, Claire," he said, his dark eyes holding hers.

"Some time ago," she said neutrally. "I decided that you must be dead. Yet here you are."

"In the flesh, so to speak." His warm brown eyes moved over her in kind judgment.

"You look healthy." Claire kept her eyes on his face, refusing to make her own appraisal, to acknowledge the warmth that now flowed through her. "So what have you been up to?"

"Living up to my reputation, mostly. I was in the navy," he said, "and then I did some traveling. A lot of traveling, actually. But I've been back in the States for about four years. I heard you got married." He smiled crookedly, accenting a small scar on the left side of his jaw.

"And divorced."

"I heard that, too. How are you?"

"How do you expect me to be after all that's happened here?"

"Stupid question, I guess. Walter will be all right." He reached out to touch her shoulder lightly. "Don't worry about him."

"Back on farm business, Dan?" She turned away from his consoling hand, suddenly wanting to avoid his touch.

"I heard about Walter and decided to come take a look for myself." He leaned against a table, catching her with his disconcertingly direct gaze.

"And you arrived here the very next day? You heard the news pretty fast, didn't you?"

"I was in the area." He picked up a delicate china cup painted in a wild rose pattern, studying it casually. "When will the shop be open again?"

"I don't know." Claire watched him turn the cup in his broad hands. He handled it with a tenderness seemingly foreign to those long, strong fingers. "That depends on when Walter is healthy enough to run the place, I guess. If it ends up being a long recuperation, we may not be open for quite a while. I'm doing an inventory now, and I don't want to open for business until it's finished."

"You'll be open before Christmas, though," Dan said. "Emily Hoffner's antiques are an ingrained part of many holiday traditions around here."

"I sure hope we'll be open, but everything is up in the air right now." Claire leaned back against a low washstand, watching the man as he studied the wares around him. He was doing nothing out of the ordinary, only standing slightly on one leg with one hand tucked into the pocket of his jeans while he smoked and looked casually at the antiques.

"You're looking good, Claire. I should have kept in touch," he said quietly. "But things got in the way."

"I know. One day's priorities become dim memories so quickly," she said, and the words seemed laced with a bitterness she hadn't known she had been harboring. "Over twelve years, Danny. What happened to the time?"

"It blew away." His voice sounded small and sad as his eyes dimmed to a dull, lifeless brown. "We live our lives and it just goes."

Claire felt a small twinge of regret tighten her stomach. Time had gone, but she was surprised to realize that after all the years since high school her old feelings of hurt at his departure still lingered.

He looked at her closely, pressing his lower lip against his teeth in a characteristic gesture. Then he looked away quickly, saying, "Walter has many beautiful things here. Which one of them do you think the thief was after?"

The question surprised Claire, and she paused a moment before answering while he stared through the glass of the tall hutch in which the small china figures were kept.

"I haven't got any idea—"

"Excuse me, do you have an ashtray?" He cut her off as he turned with the butt of his cigarette burning between his fingers.

"A whole box full." Claire went behind the counter and brought out a small copper tray with a depiction of Niagara Falls stamped into its bottom. She handed it to him, and he stubbed out his cigarette and put the tray aside on the counter.

"Should quit these things," he commented. "You were saying?"

"Saying? Oh, yes, I was just going to say that I don't know what anyone would be after in here, though I'm keeping an eye out for anything unusual. The more I look the more I'm convinced that none of these pieces is so rare that it would be worth stealing, and there was two hundred dollars in the safe untouched when the police arrived.''

"Yes, I heard that the safe wasn't touched. It might have been some kid breaking in for kicks. Maybe it was accidental.''

"No, you don't accidentally pick up a heavy crock and smash somebody over the head with it. Besides, I'd hate to think it was a local boy out for fun. Think of how he would feel now.''

"And I don't suppose local kids are very good at picking locks,'' Dan mused, concentration puckering his strong brow. "Those crocks beside the wall over there. Are they the only ones in the shop?''

"I believe so,'' Claire answered slowly, considering whether she'd seen any others. "I haven't been through everything yet, though, so there might be more. How did you know about the lock being picked?''

"I took a look before coming in. He left a couple of small scratches. I see what you mean about an accident. The crocks are all stacked on the floor, and I was thinking that it might have fallen off a shelf to strike him.''

"You wouldn't display something that heavy on a tall shelf. A customer might get hurt trying to get it down.''

"Of course.'' Dan walked slowly along the display toward the front of the shop, stopping at the pyramid of crockery. "Could the thief have been after one of the crocks?''

"Come on, those old things?'' Claire scowled slightly, following him to the crockery display by the front door. "The stoneware craze ran its course long ago, and even at its height the crocks weren't so expensive that someone would break into a store to steal them."

"I guess not. So, what was he after when your uncle caught him here?"

"I don't have any idea. And I have even less idea why you should be so interested in specifics." The conversation seemed useless. Neither one of them was in a position to do anything about the break-in or Walter's condition, and she wanted him to leave her alone. "Is there a reason for these questions?"

"Of course there is," he said calmly.

"That's good. But you haven't told me what the reason is," Claire pointed out with mild sarcasm. "Is it habitual for you to be secretive?"

"Yes, a dirty habit." His smile broadened like a shield raised between them. "I thought maybe I could help find out what happened to Walter. So I've been taking a look around."

"We've got a sheriff's department to handle that."

"Sure, but they've got to patrol the whole county. I can afford to specialize."

"Okay, let's try to get everything straight. You're in the area to see how Walter is doing, and while you're in the neighborhood you plan to lend a hand in the investigation. Am I right so far?"

"On the money." Dan laughed. "Sounds a little bit odd, doesn't it?"

"More than a little bit."

"It's not odd at all, really." He leaned against the counter with his arms crossed, gazing at her seriously. "Walter did a lot for me when I was a kid. You know that. He taught me things I needed to know, helped me learn to stand on my own two feet, and I never thanked him properly for it. He was a hell of a lot more like a father to me than my own father was, and I guess I feel that I owe him something. So, if I can do anything at all to find out who put him in the hospital and help bring the man in, I want to do it. That's all.''

"Walter trusted you," she said, simply.

"Which is more than most people around here did."

"He's a good man."

"Damn right. And I don't like the idea of someone just walking in here and bashing him on the head. I plan to do something about it."

"I don't suppose Uncle Burt will be too happy with civilian help, though," Claire pointed out. "Especially your help."

"He's not your uncle," Dan replied.

"No, but what I call him has nothing to do with the fact that he is the law here, and that he'll see your snooping as interference. You don't want to open up old squabbles between you two after all this time, do you?"

"I'm not terribly concerned about that. I'm just worried about Walter." He pressed his lips into a frown. She felt a jolt of feeling, feelings she had thought long gone. He looked handsome to her, even more so than her memory of him recalled.

"Of course," she said, swallowing down the swell of emotion. "I guess Burt can't begrudge you for wanting to help. Do you have any training at criminal investigation?"

"All it takes is common sense," he said, straightening his broad shoulders. "Where was he found?"

Why shouldn't he know? she mused. She nodded to a corner. "By the counter. He managed to call for help.

The police found a magnifying glass near the site, oddly enough."

Dan didn't act as if he absorbed the information. "Have they figured out where he was when the thief hit him?"

"By that display case over there." Claire pointed at a long glass case about five feet from the checkout counter. "But I don't see how it helps to know that."

"It takes a lot of little pieces to make a whole clue." He walked over to the case, staring down at the floor. "Sure, here's some chips of crockery. This site must be twenty feet from the crockery by the front door. Did the cops take away the weapon?"

"Yes."

Dan plucked at his lower lip with his teeth as he looked around the shop. "We'll have to put our heads together on this one, Claire. If you'll let me help, that is."

"Why should I object?" She sat back against an unpainted bureau, folding her arms across her chest.

"I don't know. I was afraid you might still be mad at me."

"After twelve years? Don't flatter yourself, Dan." She laughed, trying to ignore the flutter she felt in her stomach. "I don't have any problem with our past and don't see why it would be hard for us to get along for a couple of days."

"Good."

"Why don't you go away for the moment and let me get to work counting the stock." His presence was perplexing her, confusing her emotions over Walter's condition with long gone feelings about their high school love.

"I'll be back," he said, turning toward the door without further prompting.

"You've said that before, Danny." A flash of unbidden anger pushed the words out before Claire knew what she was saying.

"Yes, I did, didn't I?" He walked to the door, then stopped. "I see they've got the old theater going again. Maybe we could take in a movie."

"Maybe." That answer surprised her almost as much as her sudden anger.

"I'll see you later, Claire. Bye."

Claire watched the door close behind him, shutting out the chill wind that had swirled in.

There was no point in wondering about the feelings his presence had stirred in her. Daylight was wasting, and she planned to visit Phillip and Janet's farm to take them up on the dinner invitation. No matter what she said about staying here, she didn't want to eat alone in her uncle's home.

Before that, however, there was one thing she had to do. She picked up the phone and dialed the number of the hospital.

The news hadn't improved: Walter's condition was the same, no change for better or worse, and the doctor could offer no hope for early recovery. She hung up the phone with tears stinging her eyes and falling over her ivory cheeks. The thought of a world without Walter Hoffner twisted her stomach into a hot knot.

You can't die, Walter. You simply can't.

Wiping away the tears, she moved to lock the front door. Something outside caught her eye, and she turned back quickly to see the same dark sedan parked across the street earlier now pulling away from the curb, the driver's face obscured by shadow.

DANIEL GARNER LAY on the bed in his room at the Red River Motel and stared up at the ceiling. He had thought that his visit to the sheriff's office in town was the hardest thing he'd ever had to do, but talking to Claire Hoffner had been.

Why couldn't she have grown ugly or remained married, with four or five kids tossed into the bargain? Why did she have to remain so beautiful? No, she'd lived up to the memories he'd stored away. Her eyes were the most beguiling green he'd ever seen; the lips, still full and ready to smile; her hair, the silken fall of auburn he'd remembered. Worse, his thoughts still became hopelessly entangled whenever he looked at her.

He hadn't counted on being thrust together with her by a coincidence that hampered his ability to be completely honest with her. He hadn't counted on looking like an unrepentant bastard after all this time.

The telephone rang, and he grabbed it and growled his greeting into the receiver.

"Yeah?"

"What have you found out?" his caller asked tersely.

"Nothing yet. The thief may have been after the crockery. Other than that, I don't have anything. What about Claire Hoffner? I think she should be brought into this to a certain degree."

"That call is up to you, Garner, but I'd advise against it. Even if she's not connected, she might talk and warn your suspect. We've been after these guys too long to have anything go wrong now."

"I'm not worried about that, but I don't want to get her involved too deeply. It could get dangerous. What about the Minneapolis end?"

"No leads. The clues all died at the art gallery. We've got to get a break on this thing soon," Peters continued. "These people have been operating much too long. It's beginning to be an embarrassment to the department. We can't take any chances at losing them now. Besides, we're taking a lot of heat about it here."

"It's about time you felt some of the pressure, Peters. What about Hans? Have you picked up his trail again?"

"No, we lost him in Winnipeg. I think your ideas about Hans Wermager are screwy anyway. Just because he was on the end of the pipeline once, doesn't mean he's there all the time."

"That's not what you thought when you put me back into the field to chase him," Dan replied angrily. "I'm supposed to be a civilian by now."

"You will be. We've circulated your new police file to European law enforcement agencies. We'll revise your domestic status as soon as this one is wrapped up. So wrap it up, buddy. And don't trust anyone."

"I don't." Dan twisted his lips sourly, realizing how that simple truth summed up his life. "And that's why I want out. I'm tired of lying and sneaking around and feeling more like a criminal than the criminals I'm stalking. This isn't the kind of occupation a man can continue in forever."

"I appreciate that, Dan, and you'll get your discharge as soon as this is finished. But until then, play it by the book."

"You just find Hans and dig up something in Minneapolis. I'll take care of my end."

He hung up the phone and stood. This was no good. Even if he knew how to explain his life to Claire, the twisted logic of his job made it difficult to do so. And when Sheriff Burt Peterson decided to get curious and run a check on Dan's past, as he surely would, he'd find all those tidy little criminal charges and suspicions about him scattered along the eastern seaboard. They'd been planted long ago by the department. There'd be no explaining after that.

But why did he feel it was necessary to explain anything? He didn't need to justify his life to her. Or did he? Seeing her again had jumbled his thoughts too much to know for sure.

He opened his suitcase and withdrew a compact black revolver in a belt holster. He checked it over quickly and then put the weapon back into the suitcase and turned out the lights. Then he set his travel alarm for midnight and laid back on the bed fully clothed. It was going to be another long night.

Chapter Three

It was the sound of the wind that first woke her, for it was rushing around the downtown buildings with a freight train shriek. It had gained force while she slept, fluctuating in pitch as it rattled the wooden sign hanging from the front of the shop. It was nearly one a.m.

Claire rolled listlessly in the single bed beneath the window in Walter's guest room, not immediately aware of where she was. Then she fixed her gaze on the lighted rectangle behind the thin curtains over the bed, watching the curtains moving slightly in the draft that forced itself through the old window. She could hear the rattle of icy snow beating on the panes. The winter that had been postponed briefly had arrived.

She turned toward the wall and snuggled deeper beneath her covers, secure against the storm. As a child the night had been her favorite part of winter. Curling up safe and warm within her bed while the fury of nature spent itself against the old farmhouse made her appreciate her life and be extra thankful for her grandmother's thick comforter. Now she lay breathing evenly and letting that old childhood feeling of security wash over her.

But then there was a different sound, a deeper, drawn out cry of wood pressing against the restraint of the nails that bound it. And a distinct click, heard clearly through the howl of the wind rattling past the sign outside.

Claire turned and threw back the covers, shivering as she stepped softly onto the cold wood floor beside the bed and clutched her flannel nightgown to her. She'd left the bedroom door slightly ajar, and she approached it carefully, watching to avoid walking into any furniture in the dimly-lit bedroom.

A rapier-thin beam of light moved in the living room, lashing out from the dark figure of a man. Claire pressed against the door frame and peered out, watching as the man swept the light around the room.

She drew back as the light circled nearby, flashing on the bureau against the wall in the guest room. She could hear him walking toward Walter's room and the door opening.

No time for thought, Claire moved toward the kitchen. She had to sneak out and call the sheriff from the telephone in the shop below.

The beam of light slashed out and past her, glaring on the wall before her. Panicking she ran, her heart pounding, faster as she raced on. But she didn't move fast enough. Three thudding steps and he was on her, grabbing her by the shoulders and pulling her back off her feet before she'd gotten halfway through the kitchen. She fell against him, knocking him off balance into the door frame. As his grip loosened, she spun to punch her fist into his unprepared stomach and scratch his cheek.

He stepped back with a ragged gasp, but the reprieve was brief. He spun her, catching the fabric of her nightgown, stopping her in the door to the living room. She slapped back at his restraining arm without effect, then clutched the door in desperation, kicking against his legs.

"Hold it!" he snarled, his voice tight with pain. By sheer size he overpowered her, and pushed her forward to the floor, shoving her face roughly into the carpeting, and holding her with a knee pressing like a stone in the small of her back.

"Where is it?" he breathed, close to her ear.

"What?" Claire cried out as he jabbed his knee against her spine.

"Where is it?" he repeated. "My only way out now is to get it, so you'd better tell me."

"But I don't know what you want," she sputtered.

He moved his hand away from her neck and grabbed a handful of hair, which he yanked.

"Where did the old man hide it?" He tugged again. "Tell me!"

"Claire!" A second man's voice called out, echoing from the shop below. "Claire!" Footsteps rattled up the steps.

The man released her, jumping to his feet. Claire twisted and grabbed one ankle.

"Up here!" Her voice was a tight gasp.

Someone burst through the door as the man swung his leg back and broke her grip. He ran, pushing the kitchen table ahead of him at the newcomer. Claire staggered to her feet, holding the frame of the kitchen door.

The intruder had jammed the table into the doorway leading to the shop below, momentarily blocking the way. In an explosion of movement, the man lunged out the back door as the kitchen table flipped over and clattered against the steel cabinets by the sink. A dark shape crossed to follow Claire's assailant onto the wooden stairs.

A sharp popping sound ensued, followed by a flare of light as Claire ran to the outside landing. The icy wind slammed against her as she peered into the darkness below for any sign of movement. Then a car roared to life and streaked down the alley, a blur of headlights flickering past the gap between buildings. It briefly silhouetted a dark figure crouching toward the fleeing car, arm extended, firing one last shot as the vehicle sped away.

She waited, shivering against the wind, until the dark figure turned and ran back toward the steps, coming up to her two steps at a time.

"Are you all right?" It was Dan Garner, approaching with his now empty hands out as if to catch her. But he stopped one step below her, looking up anxiously. He didn't touch her.

"No," Claire said. "Come inside."

Dan entered behind her, closing the door and standing before it while she turned on the kitchen light. He was dressed just as he had been when he was in the shop earlier, and it looked as though he hadn't been to bed yet.

"What are you doing here?" Claire leaned against the wall, grateful for some solid support as she watched him. She felt numbed, and in need of answers.

"Insomnia. I got caught up in a book, and I went out to raid the pop machine at the gas station. I saw a strange car in the alley and decided to try the back door."

"There's a pop machine at the motel." His explanation was too easy and explained too much.

"I know. It ate my money."

"How did your journey to the gas station manage to take you past the back of the shop?"

"Just checking." He spoke confidently, sure of every word, but the look in his eyes betrayed a hint of uncertainty as he watched her.

"I don't need anyone checking up on me." She clenched her lips into a hard line, anger coloring her emotions now. Nobody seemed to believe that she was capable of staying alone in the apartment—not Phillip, Burt, Jimmy or even Dan. But then the thought of him taking the time to check up on her well-being broke down her antagonism, and she smiled. "I'm sorry. Thank you, Dan," she said.

"You're welcome."

They stood for a moment without speaking as a smile struggled onto Dan's sturdy features, and he shifted his weight from one leg to the other. Finally Claire released a tense sigh.

"This can't be happening," she said.

"What did he do to you?" Dan took a step into the room, drawing his hands from the pockets of his heavy jacket.

"Tried to vacuum the carpeting with my face. He wanted me to tell him where something was, but he didn't tell me what he wanted."

Anger, and something more—curiosity?—crept into his eyes.

"Could you identify him if you saw him again?"

"I didn't see his face," she said, frowning.

"What did he say to you?" He stepped closer. "What were his exact words?"

"He asked 'where did the old man hide it?' And he said something about how his only way out now was to find 'it.'"

"But he didn't say what 'it' was?"

"No." Claire watched him closely, noting the thoughtful interest on his face. "Do you know something about this?"

"No. Why?" He looked past her briefly, then returned his face to hers.

"Why should you want to know his exact words?"

"It's easier to remember them now than later. That's all. Like his voice. Did he speak with an accent. Was there anything distinct about his voice at all?"

"No accent. I wouldn't say it was distinctive in any way. Really, Dan, I couldn't identify him if he was sitting across from me. Now, what about the gun?"

"I've got a license for it." He turned away to lift the kitchen table back onto its legs, sliding it back toward the wall.

"That's not what I meant. Are you going to tell me why you have a gun? And why did you need it to go for a can of pop at the gas station?"

"I keep it in my car. When I checked the back door of the shop, it seemed smart to have it with me." He stared at her, his eyes moving down her body. "The snow is melting on you," he said. "You'd better get something dry on."

"I'd better call Burt first."

"I'll call him. You're shivering."

Claire nodded slowly but didn't acknowledge that she was shivering more out of fright than cold. The assault had been so quick and brutal that it left her dazed, but the shock was wearing off, leaving her with a knot of fear lying cold and hard in her stomach. She was afraid of the man and what he had done to her, and afraid of the reasons Dan might have for carrying a gun. But she didn't want to acknowledge her fear or admit to the fact that she longed for the comfort of his arms around her to chase her fears away.

She didn't say anything more to him, but turned and walked across the dark living room back to her bedroom.

Burt sat at the table in the small kitchen staring thoughtfully at the wall. He'd heard them both through, interrupting only once to ask about Dan's gun, and now he rubbed his bulbous nose with one thick finger and scowled.

"I thought we were done with this crap," he said at last. "I hate to think of you being in the middle of it, little missy." He regarded Claire lovingly, his gentle gaze remembering her as a child toddling into the sheriff's office calling out for Sheriff Burt in her sweet, high voice. Then he frowned, shaking his head. "Haven't had a robbery in town in years," he said. "And, I don't remember anything even vaguely resembling a crime wave in, hell, I don't know how long." He cast a significant look at Dan, who was leaning on the wall by the stove. "When were those break-ins, Danny?" he asked pointedly.

"I'd say about thirteen years ago, Burt." Anger lurked behind his dark brown eyes, and his voice was tightly controlled. "You know that very well."

"Memory ain't what it used to be, Danny," he said, pushing himself up from the table. "Anything get broken up in the struggle?" he asked, stepping through to the living room. He noticed the grandfather clock. "Your clock is a bit fast," he mentioned, consulting his watch.

"I think it needs a little work." Claire glanced at the more modern clock above the kitchen sink.

"Just another busted antique." Burt cleared his throat impatiently, then walked through the kitchen to the doors. "Let's go on down and see if anything is disturbed downstairs."

Dan waited until they passed and followed them down the stairs. The sheriff paused for a moment inside the shop, then walked over to the checkout counter.

"He's a neat burglar," Claire commented, following him. "I don't see anything out of place offhand."

Burt stopped by the cash register and leaned against it tiredly. "I took a look out back before coming up, and the way it looks, I'd say he broke in before it started to snow. That was about midnight."

"Almost forty-five minutes inside? Can you be sure of that?"

"Definite," the big man stated. "There's a big patch of dry dirt in the alley where the car stood while it was snowing, and the only tracks he left were when he tore off down the alley to get away. I can personally vouch for the time, because I was sitting in the café at midnight when it started snowing.'' The sheriff surveyed the room absently as he spoke. "Any ideas, Garner?''

"You going to dust for prints?''

"Not much use,'' Burt said. "There were no prints on the crock he clobbered Walter with, so he obviously wore gloves the first time. Probably wore them again.''

"Probably is miles away by now,'' Dan commented, looking away.

"Grumble all you want, Danny, but our hope isn't in finding prints, but for Claire to find out if anything is missing.''

"I won't be much help there right now, I'm afraid,'' Claire said. "This afternoon was the first time I'd spent in the shop since last Christmas. I've barely started.''

"Well, you take a quick look around just to see if there's anything obvious, then head on back to bed,'' Burt said, smiling kindly. "From what you told me, our man must not have found what he was looking for, anyway.''

"You're obviously dealing with a very dedicated collector here.'' Dan stopped at a table displaying antique dolls. He picked up a Kewpie doll and examined it casually.

"You think so, do you?'' Burt's tone was gruff, accusing, when he spoke to Dan. "Any other helpful ideas? Aside from tossing print dust over everything, that is.''

The tension between the two hadn't let up since Burt's arrival.

"Not offhand. You're the big crime solver here, Burt. You should have it all wrapped up in no time.''

"I might at that," the officer replied. "You know, you never really explained why you're in town, Garner."

"Yes I did." Dan put the doll down and walked to face the older man as Claire looked on. "I came to see what happened to Walter."

"You being an authority on breaking and entering and all, right?" The sheriff chuckled roughly, but he didn't smile as he regarded Dan. "Did you come to do my job for me, Danny?"

"No, you've got Jim Webster for that."

"You arrived awfully quick on the heels of the event, didn't you?"

"Bad news travels fast."

"And you brought along a gun in case we opened up a local hunting season?"

"I told you about that, Burt. I keep it in my car. The permit is in the glove box if you want to see it."

"Later. What exactly do you know about this business?"

"Not a damn thing," Dan said hotly. "Are you making some kind of accusation against me?"

"I wouldn't accuse you of anything, Danny," he answered snidely. "I'm sure you're an honest, upright citizen."

"Of course he isn't accusing you, Dan," Claire cut in. "He knows how close you were to Walter, and you have no reason to be so defensive. Now, we should get some sleep and see what we can figure out in the morning."

"Good idea." Dan smiled at her. "Maybe Burt will decide who to pin it on by then."

"You're a smart-aleck, Danny," the sheriff said, then added, in a caustic tone, "but if I do find out who did it, you can be sure you'll be the first one I notify."

"That would be damn nice of you, Burt."

The two men stood face-to-face, not more than three feet apart, and stared at each other with unmasked contempt. Something in their eyes and the set of their jaws made Claire afraid that they were going to come to blows. Then Dan let a crooked grin break his somber mask and turned to Claire.

"Nothing really changes, does it," he said for no apparent reason. "It's nice to be able to rely on the old hometown to stay exactly as you remember it."

"I suppose so." Claire glanced at Burt Peterson, but he was still watching Dan Garner with obvious dislike.

Suddenly coming to life, Burt turned to her and said, "I'll be going now, Claire." He hugged her shoulders briefly with one arm near the door. "You should be safe enough here tonight, but I'd recommend staying with Phillip and Janet tomorrow. Stop by the office in the morning to fill out some forms, won't you, honey. Good night."

"Good night, Uncle Burt. Thanks for coming." Claire called out at his back as he walked quickly out the door.

"Did I scare him off?" Dan leaned his elbows on the counter, looking up at Claire.

She turned to him, bristling. "After all these years, why can't you get along with Burt?"

"Force of habit, maybe," he said, frowning. "But that's old news."

"No, it's obviously not old news. You two had your scrapes in the past, but that was a long time ago. I can't believe you would carry a grudge so long over some juvenile misdemeanor.''

"You have too many uncles in town, Claire," Dan said, softly.

"What does that mean?"

"Nothing. I don't want to talk about it."

"No, and it's too late at night to start going over things here." She'd thrown on a pair of jeans and a gray sweatshirt, but it wasn't enough to guard against the cold air in the shop, and she hugged her arms around herself as she regarded Dan. "We'll figure this thing out somehow."

"No clues, no suspects, no motive. Do you think Dick Tracy can handle it?"

"You know I don't like you putting him down." Claire leaned across the counter, bringing her head close to his. "So cut it out. Okay?"

"Okay." Dan looked at her seriously, his dark eyes seeming to absorb her with their studious gaze. "It's late, and I've got a book to finish. Good night." He pushed himself away from the counter, turning on one heel.

"Good night, Dan."

"By the way," he said, turning as he moved toward the door. "I checked out the flick at the Roxy. It's one of those slasher movies. Not my cup of tea. Maybe we could go out to dinner."

"Are you so desperate for company?"

"Yes, aren't you?" His quizzical smile broadened beneath the hypnotic gaze of his dark brown eyes as he watched her.

"Maybe I am." Claire leaned on the counter where Dan had been, returning his appraising look in kind.

She noticed how his wide shoulders tapered to his waist; his sturdy legs. "I suppose there are worse things than dining with you."

A smile erupted on his face. "I'll take that as a yes."

"I said maybe. Let's leave it at that for the moment."

"Okay," he agreed, pleased with the light parrying. But before he left, he had to know. "Do you have any news about Walter?"

"I called tonight. No change." Worry quenched the beginnings of happiness that Dan's glib talk was forcing into her heart.

Dan didn't reply to her news but nodded his head a bit, then said, "I'll see you this afternoon, then. I wouldn't worry about checking things over tonight. I don't imagine anything will be missing. Bye now."

"Good night, Dan."

Claire leaned on the counter, watching the door swing shut against the winter wind. Despite the chill she felt warmed by his presence. As she bolted the door behind him, she wondered what that scene between the two men had been about. Dan's deep-seated antipathy toward Burt had been a sore point between them when they were dating in high school, and Burt himself had suggested many times that she avoid the wild rich boy.

Burt's comment about breaking and entering was her most likely clue to their feud. Dan had broken into some of the stores in town when he was in his junior year. Though she had never pressed him for details, she knew they were just childish pranks. He changed prices on some items and rearranged some shelves, nothing serious. And she felt certain that Phillip had been in on a couple of those forays.

But what if he'd done it again with more serious intent? Peterson's Hardware had been robbed shortly before Dan left town, and no one was ever apprehended for it. What if Dan was responsible and Burt Peterson had known? Sure, and Dan's parents had probably found some way to buy him out of the trouble, the way they'd bought him out of trouble before. That was something Burt Peterson wasn't likely to forget.

That thought quelled the comfortable feeling she'd begun to develop with Dan. Was he really as bad as Burt used to insist? Was he still?

"I've got a strong lead here, Peters. But I'm not about to act on it without corroborating evidence from the other end."

Dan sat on the edge of his bed, holding the receiver with his bare shoulder while he lit a cigarette. He'd undressed partially and turned on the television before deciding to wake his superior in Washington. An old movie was playing on the television, providing the illumination for the room.

"The good news is that our thief must be staying in the area if he's still around. I can probably pick up his trail at a motel in some nearby town." He combed his fingers through his thatch of curly hair, yawning.

"How can you be so certain that he doesn't live there already?" Peters spoke through a yawn on the other end of the line. He hadn't appreciated the perverse pleasure Dan took in waking him so early in the morning.

"Because he had to have been in on the theft to know there's anything worth stealing in the first place. Don't worry, the local angle still looks good. I'll get back to you later," he said, stifling his own yawn. "Goodbye."

He hung up the phone and walked over to turn off the television. Then he stood by the window for a moment, smoking his cigarette and watching the dying wind push through the branches of the trees across the street. It had stopped snowing, and the sky was clear—full of stars and possibilities.

But he could foresee only one possibility. Burt was going to call for his police records. It would be all too easy for the sheriff to decide to believe anything Burt said. And by the time everything was sorted out, the stolen papers would be out of the country.

Chapter Four

The sky was a slick unrelieved ceiling of gray. It hung low above the streets on Monday morning, while the wind sliced across the prairie from the north. The new snow was rough and crunchy underfoot, but ground to dirty slush in the streets by passing vehicles. Winter hadn't come in with a pretty display this year, but it was finally here to stay.

Claire made her way from the sheriff's office, where she'd signed the report of the break-in, to the shop. Her hands were thrust deep into the pockets of her down-filled coat, worn over a pair of gray wool slacks, and the wind sneaked in past her collar.

"Hey, Claire!" Jimmy Webster caught up with her at the antique store. He trotted up beside her, panting. "Had some more excitement last night, did you?"

"More excitement than I need." She opened the door and stepped in ahead of him. "What's happening in our little town?"

"You got me," he said. "Burt is nervous as a cat about it, too."

"Do you have any idea what's going on?"

"Not a one. And last night confuses the issue even further." The deputy unzipped his coat and pushed it back. He planted his hands on his hips. "Why on earth would he come back? And what was this business about Walter hiding things? Confidentially, Claire, we can't figure out what's going on."

"I don't think Burt's mind was on the case last night, anyway." Claire carried her own coat back and draped it over the checkout counter. "He was more interested in sniping at Dan than checking things out."

"Yeah." The deputy tapped one foot slowly, then walked up to the counter. "He put through a request to the FBI for a background check on Danny."

"What do you mean? He's looking for a criminal record?"

"Guess so. No, don't ask, because I don't know why." He held up his hands, laughing. "He didn't say a word about it to me. Iris filled me in."

"That's awfully strange, isn't it? If he suspects Dan of doing something wrong, he'd probably alert you to his suspicions, wouldn't he?"

"Normally, yes. But I think this is more a personal thing than official. But like I said, Burt is nervous about everything right now."

"You don't suspect Dan of being involved in the break-in, do you, Jimmy?" Claire watched the deputy closely as he frowned to himself.

"No, I don't. And frankly, I wish I did. If there was some reason to be suspicious of Dan, I'd feel a lot happier about Burt's request. You know Burt isn't the type who is prone to unfounded suspicions."

"That's what worries me." Claire leaned her hip against the counter, crossing her arms thoughtfully.

"What if he does have good reason to suspect Dan but he just doesn't want to say anything until he's sure?"

"No, not in this case." Jimmy's smile was reassuring and genuine. "Dan wasn't even in the country at the time of the assault. He was in Canada, and he had his hotel receipt and a copy of his customs declaration form dated Friday morning to prove it."

Then he leaned one hand on the counter, drumming his fingers as he looked at her with perplexed concern. "But you know, that was something strange," he said. "Dan came into the office around noon on Friday and asked us about the break-in. I told him what we had so far, pretty much bringing him up-to-date. But then Burt showed up and got testy about my telling Danny anything at all about the investigation. And then Dan said something about how he'd brought proof of his whereabouts with him in case Burt wanted to pin the crime on him. That's when he showed him the papers he brought along."

"He didn't offer to show them to you?"

"No. I had no reason to think he needed an alibi, but Dan seemed to feel he'd need one for Burt."

"What did Burt say?"

"He told Danny to go to hell." Jim laughed. "No, I'd say there's no love lost between the two of them."

"Everything is wrong here, Jim," Claire stated sadly. "The town seems the same as always, but down deep everything is wrong somehow."

"Yeah, things like this aren't supposed to happen here."

CLAIRE'S CALL TO THE hospital was greeted with the same news. He was still in a coma but holding his own, and they wouldn't be able to make any predictions about his recovery or the severity of his injuries until he woke up. If he woke up.

And across the street the dark sedan was parked at the curb once again. A late-model Chevrolet, it was parked inconspicuously enough in the line of cars waiting for afternoon shoppers downtown. She might not have noticed it at all if the man hadn't been sitting and calmly smoking a cigarette.

Dammit! This can't be happening!

Claire unlocked the door and stepped through, heedless of the chill wind swirling down the highway from the north. She walked resolutely across toward the man parked at the curb, hurrying as he caught sight of her approach and in a rush started his car.

"Wait!" she shouted, running.

She'd just gotten to the car when he popped it into gear and jerked away from the curb, swerving dangerously and deliberately close to her. She had to jump back and watch as he continued south on the highway, thwarted from getting a good look at the driver's face.

Was this the man who'd put Walter in the hospital? He had to be, just as he had to be the man who'd assaulted her in the apartment. She stood in the street staring at the illegible mud-encrusted license plate of his car, her mind swirling with new questions and possibilities. If he was still in town, still watching the shop, then there was still hope of discovering some answers.

This man meant business, and the pang of fear she'd had earlier flared in Claire's stomach again. He'd had no qualms about running Claire down—no more than he'd had about clubbing Walter.

What if Walter never woke up? she wondered, hurrying back into the store. That would almost be worse than his death. Months or years of hoping for recovery answered only by the continuing coma would be unbearable. It would be the worst fate possible.

Driven on by her anger and the memory of the man in the car, and armed with Walter's unfinished inventory, Claire was able to make quick progress with her accounting of the shop's contents. But when she got beyond his list she was left with at least a quarter of the shop unsorted and uncategorized. Just as always, he'd left the largest pieces for last, and most of them were stacked up in the back room. Still, the only way to get it done was to do it, so she forged ahead.

"Knock, knock!" Dan Garner made his way to where she was working and stood smiling over her as she sat back on her heels and pushed a silken strand of auburn hair from her face. "Having fun?" Humor radiated from the corners of his softly appraising eyes, crinkling his tanned, weatherworn skin with happy lines.

"Not particularly." She regarded him distantly, keeping her pert lips neutral as she maintained a cool attitude against her instinct to smile. No matter what else she wanted to think about him, he was still a handsome man whose smile struck a chord deep within her. "Have you done anything constructive today?"

"Maybe," he said cryptically. "How long will it take for you to get ready for dinner?"

"Dinner? I hadn't planned on stopping any time soon."

"You've forgotten our date?" He cocked his head, his expressive mouth slipping into a grin. "I was vain enough to think I made a more lasting impression than that.''

"You made a lasting impression," she said. "And not only on me. I just hope you don't have anything to hide."

"Nothing important," he said, holding out his hand to help her up. "Why?"

She accepted his hand, allowing him to pull her up toward him, and stood for a moment just inches apart, letting the warmth of his hand in hers spread throughout her body. Her heart seemed to catch as she looked into his smiling brown eyes, its palpitations drawing her back toward trust and, maybe, love. She looked away, dropping his hand.

The physical attraction was there and could not be denied, but she wasn't a schoolgirl waiting to be swept off her feet and she refused to act like one. She'd been down that road with him before.

"I was just asking," she said, taking a breath to fight the tingling sensation that continued to spark through her body after their touch. "Because Jim said that Burt has called the FBI about you. He wants to know if you have a criminal record."

"Is he looking for an excuse to run me out of town on a rail?"

"Maybe." She returned her gaze to his, her intelligent green eyes narrowing to study him. "Is he going to find one?"

Dan paused for a long moment, staring back at her without blinking. *Please say there's nothing.* Claire thought. *Please laugh it off as a minor annoyance.* But he neither laughed nor denied, and didn't explain, either.

"Yes," he said. "I expect he'll find some irregularities."

"Irregularities?" Concern knotted her fine brow as she stared at him. "What have you been up to, Dan?"

"Give me one more day, won't you?"

"Come on, Dan, is Burt going to find a criminal record?"

"Yes." Dan's face was set in a grim mask. "But it's not as bad as you think."

"It would seem that having a record is bad enough in itself," she commented wryly.

"I don't feel free to say everything I want to tell you, Claire." A pained expression clouded his eyes, and he smiled wanly. "Not yet anyway. Right now, I'd like to eat."

"I've really got to finish my inventory, Dan," she protested, deciding that finding out who hurt Walter was more important than probing this latest mystery. "I was just going to grab something quick later on."

"You don't really feel like going upstairs and cooking a TV dinner, do you?"

"No, I don't," she admitted, smiling despite herself. "But I don't think I'd be very good company, either. Not with everything up in the air like it is."

"I'm worried about him, too." His strong hands slipped into his pockets in a well-remembered gesture as his full lips compressed in thought. "But fasting won't help him get better. And an hour or two won't set your inventory back that much. Come on, I'll give you five minutes to get ready."

Feeling cheated out of some undefined victory by her own hunger, she smiled at him. "Okay. You win. I'll be right back."

Laying her inventory list aside, she went up to the apartment while he sat behind the counter and lit a cigarette. She wanted answers to her questions; she wanted explanations and apologies about the past. She could help Walter and satisfy her curiosity about Dan by sitting with him a few hours.

They dined in a booth in the Farmer's Kitchen, Garner Falls's only café. It was a comfortable place, furnished with booths and stools lined against a long lunch counter. What it lacked in decoration it made up for with the food. For over twenty years, Merle Swenson, the owner, had been serving and satisfying farmers and truck drivers and local families with his wizardry at the grill behind the small order window.

Dan opened up somewhat at dinner, though not in reference to any police record he may have had. Instead he recounted his favorite stories from his time in the navy, and before long she was laughing until tears sprang to her eyes.

She watched him over the narrow table in the booth, noticing his relaxed and articulate manner. It was his natural ease that first drew her to him just as it was drawing her now. Yes, whatever indefinable chemistry they'd had before was still there and she couldn't help but respond. Did he feel it, too?

"What about after the navy?" Claire rattled the ice in her glass of water slightly, watching the cubes swirl and wanting to be a thousand miles away rather than here with her frail feelings.

"I served four years and got out." He seemed to be focusing his eyes through her, concentrating on some point behind her head as he spoke. "I stayed in Europe then and got to know the place on my own terms by working odd jobs. I came back to the States when my grandfather died four years ago. Grandpa always liked me for some unexplained reason, and he left me a big house in Connecticut and some property that needed attention."

"So you're a landowner now?"

"Sold most of it." Dan grinned. "Not the house, of course, but all the land. That really put me in solid with the relatives. I'm no real estate baron."

"You really haven't changed, have you?" Claire commented, laughing. "Still doing whatever you like and taking the consequences as they come."

"Oh, I've changed drastically since then. My waistline has expanded by three inches, for one thing."

"That's not exactly what I meant."

"I have settled down quite a bit. Life has a way of educating even the most determined fools, Claire, and I'm not too stupid to learn." He took a sip of water, holding her eyes over the rim of the glass.

"Yes, I guess we all wise up eventually."

Their conversation was cut off by the arrival of Ginny Swenson, Merle's eighteen-year-old daughter, with their food. Claire ate with mixed emotions. Why couldn't he have gone bald or something, anything to deflect the feelings stirring within her. She didn't know if she wanted to entangle her life with love right now.

"Before Burt gets his reports back from Washington, I'd like a chance to say something, Claire," Dan said as they were finishing their meal.

"That might be a good idea." Claire's throat tightened in anxious anticipation.

"Don't judge me by what he says. I can't talk about it right now, but there is a good reason for everything.

He's going to be awfully excited by his news tomorrow, and he'll sure as hell be spreading it around town, but don't believe it."

"Are you saying that his information won't be true?"

"No. It's true enough—on paper, anyway. But sometimes the truth isn't the same as reality. And sometimes the truth can be changed."

"Come on, Dan. Either you have a criminal record or you don't."

"Sure, just like the world is flat," he said. "Or, it isn't. The truth depends entirely upon what facts are on hand."

"You have an amazing knack for making simple truths sound suspect, Garner," Claire said. "But at least you aren't boring."

"Thank God for that. If things work out, I should be free to tell all soon."

"Really, Dan, if you don't want to explain yourself you should just shut up and be done with it."

"I don't know why I'm doing this to myself," he said, frowning. "You're right, of course. All I'm doing is making myself sound like a bigger jerk than I am, and I don't really believe that I'm protecting anything. Would you be happy if I said that I work for the government and let it go at that for now?"

"Not particularly," she said with a laugh. "I'm more likely to believe you're a crook."

"I think I'll leave it at that for now."

He looked so serious then that Claire was inclined to believe him. Inclined to, but not quite ready. Still, there was no sign of deception, no break in the deadly serious set of his firm lips and unwavering eyes. There was nothing there, no lie in those eyes.

Even after all these years, Dan was unable to lie to her without giving it away in his eyes. She'd give him his time.

"So what should I be doing to help find out who beat up Walter?"

"You'll have to go over your inventory very closely, as you've indicated you will do," Dan told her. "And, pay close attention to those stoneware crocks."

"Why? Nobody would steal crocks."

"I agree. But the burglar must have been doing something with them if he had one over by that display case. A thief running away wouldn't have carried anything with him, and the shards indicate he was at least twenty feet from the other crocks when he struck Walter. He could have used any object nearby. By the way, did you find that any were missing?"

"I haven't gotten that far yet. I have to finish the new inventory so I can compare it to both his last complete inventory and his receipt book. That way I'll see what items from the old inventory were sold between then and now, and to whom."

"That's awfully complicated, isn't it?"

"Yes, but Walter hates to do book work. He always leaves it till the last minute, making it a terrible chore for anyone to undertake."

"Just count the crocks and that's all you need do," Dan said positively. "It has to be the crocks."

"Good evening, Claire."

She looked up to see Jim Webster standing by the booth with his uniform hat in one hand. He looked uncertainly at them, a small smile forced onto his lips.

"Evening, Jimmy," Dan said. "Join us for coffee?"

"Can't. On duty. You've sure got Burt up in the air, Dan," the deputy said, smiling. "What's going on with you?"

"He just doesn't want an ex-juvenile delinquent poking his nose into official business, I guess," Dan said.

"Sure." Jim laughed. "If we were to check you out, you'd turn out to be clean, wouldn't you?"

"I certainly hope so," Dan said with deep conviction. "But you never know."

"I told him about it, Jim."

"Yeah, I figured you would. I guess that's why I told you."

"Thanks for the warning, but I'm not worried about anything," Dan said.

"Good. Well, I'm going back on patrol," the deputy said. "You two have a nice evening now, okay? See you around."

"Good night," Claire called as he walked away. "I'll talk to you tomorrow." Then she turned back to Dan. "Thank you for dinner," she said.

"Are we done with our date already?"

"We didn't have a date, Dan, just dinner. I'm tired, and I've got to pack a bag to take out to Phil and Janet's tonight."

A grin stretched across his handsome features. "At least you won't be staying in the apartment again tonight," he said. "Our man was dumb enough to break in twice, so there's no sense in assuming he won't go for three times."

No, she thought, as they left the diner and headed for his car. It was foolish to make assumptions. Look at her. She'd assumed that she was cured of her love for

Dan Garner, but throughout dinner whenever he leaned toward her or smiled at her or delivered a bad joke, her heart had pulsed as if she'd just run a ten kilometer course. Though it was sadly possible that she was only headed for another emotional fall, she couldn't seem to stop her headlong rush toward it.

"DID DANNY TELL YOU anything about what he's been doing all these years?" Claire nestled back comfortably in the reclining chair in Phillip's family room downstairs.

Janet, Phillip's trim, dark-haired wife, had joined them relaxing over coffee in the cozy room, and she sat curled against her husband's chest on the long couch. "He as much as told me to mind my own business when I asked," she said.

"He didn't say anything to me, either," Phillip added. "He must have filled you in though, didn't he, Claire?"

"No, just that he'd been in the navy," she answered. The brief explanation Dan had given her both before and at dinner lingered at the tip of her tongue, but she held it back. True or not, she didn't feel it was her place to spread it around. "He wasn't very talkative."

"If he's not talking there must be a good reason, Claire," Phillip said.

They spoke awhile longer, laughing and joking about their pasts, always skirting the painful experiences or aspects that lurked in the back of Claire's mind. But as she conversed Claire couldn't help wondering to herself about Dan and Burt, about the strange tension that existed between them and the mystery surrounding

Dan's disappearance so many years before. To her surprise her bitterness and hurt still lingered after all these years, and she supposed that the longer Dan was around, the better her chances to finally lay them to rest. But it would take a moment of truthfulness from Dan to do that, and until then, a wall would separate them and keep her from opening fully to him.

Finally Janet rose and stood over her husband, smoothing his hair back. "Well, I've got to go to bed, gang. Morning comes early when you've got to drag kids out of bed for school."

"Yes, I should turn in, too." Claire stood, stretching her back out. "I'd like to go down and see your dad in the morning."

"I was planning on going. You can ride with me," Phillip offered, then added contemplatively, "I sure missed having him here tonight. It just doesn't seem right having you back in town but not Dad."

"Did the doctors tell you anything new?" Claire asked hopefully.

"No change."

"He could go either way, couldn't he?" The crystalline clarity of that dark thought chilled Claire's mind. "It's so arbitrary."

"He'll make it." Phillip spoke with grim determination marking his brow. "I'm a lot more certain of that now. I just know he'll make it. And when he wakes up, he'll be able to give them the clue to catch the man who hit him."

Claire watched them climb the stairs from the converted basement living room where she would stay the night on the sofa bed.

She found sleep slow in coming. She was restive thinking about Walter as she'd seen him last, the plastic sheet of an oxygen tent clouding his features and the ominous shadow of an IV bottle falling across his chest. He could go either way, and the doctor was waiting just like they were.

Nothing they could do.

But as she finally found the relief of sleep, she thought of a man in a dark sedan parked on the street across from the shop. And his dangerous intentions as he swerved the car toward her on his way out of town stayed with her into her dreams.

Chapter Five

As Claire was preparing for bed, Dan was already miles away. He was waiting outside a motel in Pembina, North Dakota, about forty miles away and across the Red River from Garner Falls. He hadn't been there long, only about ten minutes, when a man emerged from one of the motel units lined up in the long, L-shaped building. The man got into a dark brown Chevrolet sedan and pulled out of his parking spot. After a safe interval, Dan followed.

"Okay, Mr. Zendler, let's see where you're off to tonight," Dan said to himself in an eager whisper. "Don't disappoint me."

Dan had spent most of the day following a hunch. If the intruder at Walter's shop was free to break in once and then come back a couple of days later, it seemed logical that he was staying someplace in the area. If, as Dan assumed, he wasn't a local man, he would have to have checked into a motel. So Dan went calling on motels in towns near Garner Falls, finally striking pay dirt in Pembina.

He told the manager that he was an investigator looking for a man who'd disappeared from his home a week earlier. When he added that the man had a history of mental instability and that he might have become disoriented and wandered off without knowing what he was doing, the manager began to look nervous, admitting that there was someone there right now who'd been acting bizarre. Some more explanation and the judicious application of a couple twenty dollar bills brought out the man's name and a more detailed account of his activities while at the motel.

After cautioning the manager not to alert his guest in any way, Dan left the motel feeling certain that he was on the right track. Now he was following the man to see if he was, indeed, their suspect. So far, the man who had registered as David Zendler was living up to expectations.

The man drove across the river into Minnesota, continuing southeast on the road leading to Garner Falls. Snow blew across the road, sparkling as it fell into the path of the headlights. There was a full moon and visibility was generally good, aided by the flat and almost treeless terrain of the Red River Valley. Dan was able to let the gap between him and the man increase to over a mile to avoid being spotted. Driving a light gray Mercedes, which wasn't exactly a car designed to be inconspicuous, Dan berated himself mentally for not renting something less memorable. As they approached the town, however, he caught up with the man, staying about a block away as he drove through to the other edge of the small town. When the man he'd identified as David Zendler stopped in the shadows of a maple grove near the older homes in town, Dan continued driving past into the country.

He turned at the first crossroad, pausing for a moment, then circling back to town.

Zendler had left his car, and Dan parked nearby. Grabbing a flashlight on the seat next to him, he went to the now-empty vehicle. Quickly and noiselessly, he checked the automobile registration in the glove box. Zendler lived in St. Louis Park, Minnesota. After rummaging through other items, Dan returned to his own car and drove a safe distance away.

Fifteen minutes later, Zendler emerged empty-handed from a sedate Victorian house that stood by the snow-swept fields on the edge of town. He started his car and drove away with Dan following after a reasonable wait. A couple of miles out, he turned onto a gravel road that led to a farmstead sheltered against the prairie by a stand of tall pines.

Dan drove past, noting that the man had parked near the yard and entered the house. Dan entered the machinery yard that was kept separate from the private grounds of the farmyard.

Ten minutes later, a light came on in the lower rear part of the house. A door slammed and the dark figure of a man ran toward the car. Another pursued, stopping in the yard as he watched the intruder's car leap to life and roar away. Dan put his own car into gear and followed, less cautiously this time.

David Zendler didn't make any more stops and drove directly back to the motel in Pembina, apparently unaware of Dan who stayed behind all the way.

"Got you now, buddy," Dan said with a laugh as he pulled in the parking lot of the motel moments after his quarry. He turned off his ignition and waited until the light came on in Zendler's room. Then he walked up to the door and knocked.

"Yeah?" Zendler called out suspiciously from inside. "Who is it?"

"Open up, Dave," Dan called. "Hans wants to talk to you."

"Get away from here!" Zendler sounded scared now, and there was a scuffling movement inside the room. "I've got nothing to say to him."

"He wants to know why you screwed up the deal, Davie." This was taking too long. Something was going to happen soon. Dan removed his gun from the pocket of his jacket, waiting for a reply.

The light inside went out just as the door flew open and a suitcase swung out to slam into Dan's stomach. The man followed, grasping Dan by the collar of his coat and spinning him against the wall. Before Dan could rise or defend himself, Zendler picked up the suitcase and used it like a hammer to bounce Dan's head against the door frame. Dan sank to the pavement in a crouch, shaking his head and groaning while Zendler ran to his car and started it.

Dan sat on the cold sidewalk and watched the man drive away. He was smiling as he slipped his gun back into his pocket. After a couple of moments, he got up slowly and returned to his own car. Then he drove back to his motel room in Garner Falls.

"Run a check on David Zendler for me," he said into the phone. He'd taken time to shower and was standing wrapped in a towel, brushing back his damp hair as he spoke. "He lives in St. Louis Park. That's a suburb of Minneapolis. Yeah, warrants, the whole bit. I'm about to lose my effectiveness here, Peters. The sheriff

has already called for my record, and he's sure to have
it by morning. I'm certain there's a well placed go-
between in Garner Falls, but I'm not certain who that
is yet. At any rate, I think we can solve it from Zendler's end of the pipeline. I'm flying to Minneapolis tomorrow. Goodbye, Peters.''

He hung up the phone scowling, then turned out the
lights. He slipped naked beneath the sheets to fall into
the deep sleep of total exhaustion. Tomorrow was going
to be the hardest day of all.

"GOOD MORNING, CLAIRE. Sleep well?''

Claire jumped slightly, turning away from the door
of the shop to face Dan Garner, who'd come up behind her as she unlocked the front door on Tuesday
morning. He was standing less than a foot behind her
with his hands in his coat pockets and his eyes moving
over her face.

"Yes, I slept very well,'' she answered, the nylon
collar of her down coat brushing her chin as the light
wind bit through the fabric of her comfortable old
jeans. Their breath rolled through the cold air, min-
gling like an icy storm cloud between them. "Do you
always sneak up on people like that?''

"Always. Open the door, it's cold out here.'' He
shrugged the coat closer to his throat.

"I'm not open for business yet,'' she said, turning the
key in the lock. "I'm going with Phillip to see Walter
this afternoon, and I've got too much work to do before then to spend time chatting.''

They stepped into the shop, pulling a crystalline fog
in with them, and Dan closed the door against the cold.

"I didn't realize I was just anyone." He unbuttoned his coat, following her back to the checkout counter.

Claire draped her coat over the glass counter and rested one hand on the cash register. "You're not."

"Good, because the kind of games that are being played in this town right now are beginning to bother me. I need someone who can help me think." He reached inside his coat and patted the breast pocket of his shirt, scowling when the hand came away empty. "Out of cigarettes," he said.

"What on earth are you talking about?"

"You haven't heard? I thought the jungle drums would have spread the news a bit more efficiently than that." He patted his jacket pockets, too, but his search was futile. "Two houses were broken into last night. Connie Sanderson's old museum and Lloyd Albertson's farm."

"Connie Sanderson? That's terrible!" Mrs. Sanderson was a widow in her seventies who lived in a large old farmhouse on the edge of town. "Was she harmed?"

"No. She slept through the whole thing." He leaned on the counter. "Probably wouldn't have noticed anything was wrong, but he had to break a window in her kitchen door to get the chain unlatched. Then she found a few things out of place when she looked around more closely. They haven't decided what the thief was after yet, but he didn't touch the silver or any of her jewelry. Lloyd Albertson heard someone in his house about two a.m., but couldn't get his pants on fast enough to catch him. Saw him running across the farmyard, though. Now Burt has two more things to scratch his head about."

"Why does it have to be the same man who's been in the shop? It might be unrelated."

"If the break-ins are unrelated, then Garner Falls is having a crime spree." He leaned one forearm on the counter between them, lowering his eyes to meet hers. "Nothing was stolen from either Mrs. Sanderson or Albertson, just like there was nothing taken here."

"I'm not sure anything was taken from here, Dan," Claire said, feeling puzzled and confused.

Dan ignored her pensiveness. "You will be because that's the only way it makes sense. Our man didn't find anything here, so he's spreading out. Our problem is to find what he's looking for."

"I haven't finished the full inventory, Dan," Claire said.

He looked grim. "Have you counted the crockery?"

"Are you still on that?" Claire walked around and took the pages she'd been working on from the drawer of her uncle's desk. "There's no way on earth that the thief was after any of the stoneware."

"Why not?"

"Because you don't steal—oh, I suppose it's possible. But your hunch seems farfetched to me."

"You do realize that the point of your inventory isn't to do an inventory, don't you? The reason is to find out what the thief was after. And one man would not sneak in here to haul off a chest of drawers."

"Okay! That's enough." Claire dropped her sheets on the counter and leveled her gaze on him. "You're just as mule-stubborn as ever, aren't you? But you aren't the elected sheriff here. Why should I assume you're more qualified than Burt to investigate this?"

"Don't assume that Burt has got all the answers on this one, Claire." He laid his arms atop the cash register, lacing his fingers together and resting his chest against them. "I've got a fair amount of experience."

"Ah, yes, you work for the government," Claire sneered. "And I'm supposed to believe you? You haven't even flashed a badge at me yet."

"Sorry. I work undercover. And, for that matter, I'm not even here in an official capacity."

"Don't tell lies, Dan. Assuming that any of this is true, you are officially here. Why else would you get so deeply involved? And why else would I get the impression you need permission to talk to me about it? Come on, Dan, you've already broken your silence, go the rest of the way." He had promised to tell her everything about himself eventually, but she needed to know now before she could take another step toward trusting him again.

He didn't say anything but walked back through the display items, examining them distractedly, then turned back toward her. "Yes, I am here officially. I'd rather not get into it too deeply, though."

"You're here officially to investigate a break-in at an antique store in a small town?" Claire scoffed, walking around the counter. "What kind of governmental interest could there be in this?"

"I don't want to get you involved in it, Claire."

"I am involved! This is my uncle's store we're talking about here. Walter is in the hospital because of this! Other people are getting drawn into it because of what happened. Why can't you tell me what's going on?"

"I—" He paused a second, frowning. "I guess I'm just used to running things by my rules."

"And what are your rules?"

"I don't really know the rules anymore." He picked up the old telephone, still unsold after so many years, and clicked the cradle a couple of times. "Don't trust anyone, I guess. Don't trust and don't talk."

"That's a sad way to live." Claire watched him as he stared at the telephone in his hand. "If that's the kind of job you have, why do you do it?"

"It's just something that I got into." He put the telephone down and approached her. "There is no easy way to get out."

He touched her shoulder, running his hand down over her arm tenderly as he gazed into her eyes. There was sadness in his eyes, sadness and a deep longing, and Claire felt sorrow as she looked at him. But she couldn't get drawn into sentimentality about the past. She felt a growing urgency to understand what happened to Walter, and after that, what had happened to Dan so many years before. She shrank away from him and folded her arms across her chest.

Dan sighed as if hearing her thoughts. "I don't know the exact connection this shop has to my case yet, Claire, but there seems to be one. And if there is, then this little shop is connected to some very dangerous people."

"Protecting me isn't going to solve the problem." She peered at him, not knowing how her appearance ruffled his composure, made him think thoughts he shouldn't now. "I think I deserve an explanation," she said.

"Oh, hell," he said with a sigh. She was right. She had a right to know because of her town roots and her ties to Walter. He'd been meaning to tell her eventually when he was more certain about the Garner Falls link to the international smuggling ring and when he was sure she was out of danger. Hell, he hated to admit it, but he still cared about her. And he hadn't wanted to tip her off too soon in case by mistake she tipped off the wrong people in a casual conversation.

"Okay, Claire," he said. "Let's just say that some documents were stolen and several of them appeared in Canada recently in a shipment of antiques purchased at this shop. I've got to find the remaining document and uncover the people who smuggled them through this shop."

"Documents?" Claire stared at him for a moment, then shook her head slowly as realization crept in. "Could this have anything to do with a recent theft in Minneapolis?"

"Maybe."

"And the break-ins are directly related to these documents that maybe were stolen in Minneapolis?"

"Possibly."

"Maybe. Possibly. Don't you have any answers?"

"I don't need any. You're quite able to figure it out for yourself."

"So you believe the Revolutionary War documents left the country through this shop. But why the break-ins? If they've established a pipeline, they wouldn't need to commit a burglary to get the goods."

"That's what we have to find out."

Claire pressed her lips together and thought about this. Deciding that cooperation was the best way to help Walter, she returned to the counter and lifted a yellow pad. Columns of densely-packed figures ran down the page and she had to take a moment. "All right. We currently have a grand total of thirty crocks in the shop," she said, finding the spot. "There are two of the big ones, twenty gallons, one ten-gallon, eight five-gallon size, ten three-gallon, and nine of the two-gallon crocks."

"Walter was clobbered with a two-gallon crock?"

"Yes."

"Now we're getting someplace," Dan said. "So that means there should be ten of the two-gallon-size crocks, but the tenth one got broken."

"That's right."

"So how do you check on your count?"

"I'll have to take the inventory book where he records everything he purchases for the shop and compare that with his receipts until I account for the items we're looking for. I should probably have his last complete inventory, too. He forgets to list things sometimes, so it would be best to have as many lists as I can get my hands on."

"Sounds like fun," he said with a small moan.

"You invited yourself into this mess, not me." Claire sat at the desk and opened the long drawer above the leg well and started rummaging through the papers stuffed inside. "I should have found his last inventory to begin with, but Walter's filing system is somewhat discouraging."

Dan pulled a chair up at her side as she closed the drawer and opened the top drawer on the right side.

"I'd imagine that the most recent physical inventory was probably last January, so it's likely to be found at the bottom of a drawer. You could go through his inventory and receipt books while I'm looking. They're in the drawer under the cash register."

Dan stood and pulled out the drawer built into the back of the display case under the register. There was a large gray ledger book in the drawer along with half-a-dozen pens and a couple scraps of paper.

"There's only one book in here, a gray one marked Purchases. Is that the one you meant? Or did you mean for me to look in the register drawer?" He hit the No Sale key and pulled the handle on the side. The drawer popped open with a ding, and Dan removed the coin tray. "Nope, nothing in here."

"There should be two books in the drawer in the display case." Claire got up to help him. "I'm sure they were here on Sunday."

"There's only one book here now," he said, motioning at the drawer.

"I saw them both. This is his inventory book, where he marks down items purchased for the shop during the year and is supposed to make a note when things are sold. The one I wanted is a large red book with sales receipts and carbons."

"Well then I was wrong," Dan said, regarding her with thoughtful eyes. "Our thief did take something out of the shop."

Claire's eyes widened in understanding and horror. "And then he went calling on Connie Sanderson and Lloyd Albertson." Despite herself, a chill swept up her spine. Their burglar was a thief after all, a desperate one.

"ALL I SAW WAS A dark form racing across the yard, Claire. Darn near broke my neck getting my pants on in the dark, which is probably what tipped him off to hit the road." Lloyd Albertson spoke with a good humor that belied the topic they were discussing. He was a thin man in his early fifties, rawboned and worn to a leathery toughness by years of sun and wind. "Couldn't describe him if my life depended on it. Except of course to say he was a fair sprinter. He crossed from the gate to the toolshed in less time than it takes to tell about it."

"How did he get in?" Dan spoke up from where he stood at the window looking at the intruder's exit path. He turned and walked back to join Claire and Albertson, who were seated on a floral couch in a living room filled with family pictures and sports trophies. "Did he leave any sign?"

"Jimmy Webster claims it was the kitchen door, but you can't prove it by me. I couldn't say for sure if the door was even locked or not."

"We were wondering about something else, Lloyd," Claire said. "Did you buy anything at Walter's shop recently?"

"Hell, I don't know." He cocked his head slightly as he thought, then tapped one thin knee with broad-knuckled hand. "Yeah, I think Marion picked something up there a while back. Can't think of what it is, though. Marion!" he called out.

"You don't have to raise the roof, I was only in the kitchen." A pleasant woman in slacks and blouse joined them. She was slim, sparrowlike in physique and demeanor, and she entered the room with a cheerful smile on her open face. After greetings, she asked, "What do you want?"

"Didn't you buy something from Walter Hoffner a couple weeks back, honey? Seems like I remember something new that you bought."

"Of course I did, Lloyd." Then she addressed Claire, saying, "He's got a memory like a sieve. I bought a Nippon figurine for Betty Hannaford's birthday and one of those cute ceramic dolls, those Kewpie dolls. I put that in my china case. And I picked up a couple of crocks to match the one your aunt gave me years ago. I started coleus in both of them."

"What size crocks were they?" Dan asked, excitement hurrying his words.

"Two gallons, both of them." She seemed somewhat taken aback by his enthusiasm, but smiled. "I've got them in the kitchen if you want to take a look."

"Yes, we'd like that," Claire said, barely able to restrain her own excitement.

They followed the woman back to the bright modern kitchen where she had two crocks sitting on a sideboard to get the full benefit of the morning light. The containers had been filled with dirt and partially filled with purple-leaved plants.

"Are they the real thing?" Dan asked, leaning down to peer at the design stamped onto the grayish-white clay.

"Yes, definitely. See here?" Claire pointed at the stencil of a redbird's wing on the side of the crock below the gracefully drawn 2 and above the company name. "The size of the wing helps to pin it down to an approximate date. They went to smaller wings around 1920." Claire stroked the pot tenderly, tilting her head to catch the light on the side, "It's too bad about this nasty scratch through the wing here," she said. "It's perfect otherwise."

"What scratch?" Mrs. Albertson scurried over and leaned down beside Claire and Dan. "They weren't scratched when I bought them."

"Right here." Claire indicated a deep scratch running over the tip of the wing.

"That's odd. And there's a scratch in this one, too," Mrs. Albertson said, looking closely at the matching container sitting on the other end of the cabinet.

There was, indeed, a scratch on the wing of the second crock, and it was in almost the exact location as the first. Claire nearly shouted out her excitement at seeing the scratches. It wasn't likely that the crocks had been damaged while sitting in the kitchen, for the scars were both deep enough to have required no small amount of force to make them. This had to be the clue they were looking for.

"When did you buy the crocks?" Dan asked, straightening up and regarding the woman.

"A couple of weeks ago. I can check that, though." Mrs. Albertson went to the kitchen table and removed her checkbook from a large sack purse hanging over the back of one of the chairs. "November twenty-second," she told them. "I stopped in on Sunday afternoon shortly after church. We went to the café that day, and I left Lloyd to talk shop while I walked down to get that gift for Betty."

"You're sure the crocks weren't scratched when you bought them?" Claire asked.

"Of course," Mrs. Albertson answered. "I wouldn't have bought damaged goods."

"I'd be happy to replace these crocks. We don't want our customers dissatisfied."

"Heavens no, dear. Like I said, Walter didn't sell me any damaged crockery. Those scratches must have happened here."

"It sounds like your thief is responsible for the scratches," Dan said.

Mrs. Albertson turned pensive a moment, then sighed. "Maybe. But I don't expect to replace them. They're like old friends by now."

Claire and Dan smiled, and promised to get back to them once the full story was pieced together. As they hurried to Dan's car, Claire turned to him. "Why do you suppose the thief left those scratches?"

"Because," he said, helping her into her side of the car, "he was looking for fake pottery."

As he slammed the door, Claire's eyes lit up. Then they dimmed. He scrambled into the car and turned on the engine, not noticing her chameleon reactions. "But couldn't he tell by looking at it whether it was fake or real?" she asked.

Dan shook his head. "Our man isn't an expert like you. He was probably checking to see if there was no overglaze, which would indicate fakery."

"That's right," she cried. "The authentics would have both an under and an overglaze because the craftsman would want to fix the design into the pot."

He saw the admiration in her eyes, and smiled. "I didn't sleep through or disrupt all my classes, Claire."

She laughed and reached over to squeeze his hand, quickly replacing her hand in her lap to ignore the electricity that passed between them. "But our man came up empty-handed again," she said.

Dan grew pensive. "That's right. He discovered the pots were authentic, not the fakes that hid the stolen contraband."

She sighed. "It's not over then. More people could be hurt."

Silence filled the car.

"Maybe we should stop by the sheriff's office, Dan, before we talk to Connie," she said as they drove through the light haze of drifting snow back toward town.

"We called before coming out here. If he's back, then he's gotten the message. If not, then stopping by won't do any good."

"And I think you want to beat him to the punch, anyway," she said.

"Damn right!" Dan laughed and pressed down the accelerator, glad for the lighter moment. "Now that we know what to ask, it shouldn't take but two minutes to confirm our theory in full."

"And then what?"

"We'll figure something out."

IT TOOK LONGER THAN two minutes at Connie Sanderson's house to finally get around to the point of their visit. The elderly woman spent the first ten minutes catching up on their activities since leaving town, asking probing questions in the manner of a newspaper reporter. In fact, she had been the town correspondent for the *Northstar Times* for fifteen years, reporting the births and deaths and other items affecting Garner Falls for the local weekly. It was clear that she hadn't lost her touch since retiring ten years earlier.

They did get to the subject of her break-in, however, and she came right to the point.

"Yes, young man," she said, when Dan asked her about purchasing a crock. "I bought a stoneware crock on the morning of the twenty-fifth of November. I remember because—well, I don't suppose it matters why I remember, just that I do."

"This crock?" Claire asked, kneeling by a vessel that stood on the floor with magazines in it.

"Yes, that very one."

"Did you notice if it was scratched when you bought it?"

"It wasn't scratched," she said positively.

"It is now, I'm afraid." And Claire looked at Dan with hopeful triumph in her eyes. They knew what the thief was after. They also knew the thief was coming up empty-handed with every fresh foray and might be growing more desperate and dangerous. Claire was now eager to find further clues and the identity of the thief himself before anyone else got hurt.

"THAT TIES IT ALL together," Dan said happily. He was rocking contentedly on a mission oak rocking chair near the checkout counter at the store.

"But it doesn't explain anything at all." Claire sat on the edge of her uncle's desk scowling at him. "You still don't have any proof of smuggling, or any sign of the missing contraband."

"You're right. We need more solid evidence, but at least we're getting closer. We know that a crock is being sought after by someone desperate, very likely the same man who hurt your uncle. And we know it probably played a key role in transporting a stolen shipment of archival treasures.''

Claire lifted a hand to her brow in exasperation, and sighed. "Dan, I need to know more background. It still doesn't make a lot of sense to me."

"Fair enough." Dan shrugged, smiling. "Some of the documents that were stolen from the Walker Art Center showed up in Canada. We suspect one or two international collectors of being behind thefts of historical documents over several years but haven't had a chance to pin down names. Until now, anyway. I did my own late-night search of an antique store in Winnipeg and found one of the stolen documents. It was smuggled out of the country in a batch purchase of antiques that came through this store. From leads, we have learned that Hoffner's Antiques served as a midway point for some time. The documents are stolen from a number of sites, packed into antiques and sold to Hoffner's. A buyer comes in knowing which batch items to buy then drives across the border into Canada. He drops them off at the next shop in the link—a shop in Winnipeg—and slowly they make their way to the end of the conduit in Europe."

"What kind of antiques did they use to smuggle out those other things?" Claire lifted her feet up onto the desk's swivel chair and then rested her elbows on her slim knees as she watched him with interest.

"A property deed with Thomas Jefferson's name on it came through hidden in the false bottom of an old washstand," Dan said. "I didn't have time to search when I was there, but the other antiques must have concealed something as well."

"Why don't the police just question the person who brought the washstand out of the country? Why go through all this cloak-and-dagger business down here?"

"We don't want to do anything to scare them into hiding."

"Who's 'them' Dan? You don't even know the identity of the man who clobbered Walter."

Dan pressed his lips together. "Yes I do, and so do you, Claire. The same man who broke into the Albertson's and Sanderson's."

"But who is he?"

"I think a man named Zendler."

Claire studied Dan a moment, wondering if he was hiding any other secrets from her. "Zendler? Zendler who? And Dan, if you know anything about who hurt Walter, how can you not go to the police..."

Dan raised his hand. "I know you're upset about your uncle, but until we figure out exactly how Zendler fits into the picture, we can't risk altering the smugglers by alerting the police. All I know is that on a hunch after your uncle's assault, I called motels and located the man. I followed him from his place and watched him drive into Garner Falls and do his number on the Albertsons."

Claire looked appalled. "But why didn't you tell me this earlier? Why... why..."

Dan reached down and grasped Claire's arms as she leaned forward in her chair. "Because there are bigger fish to fry. We've had reports that the chief architect of the smuggling ring, a man named Hans Wermager, has been seen. He was recently spotted in Canada, and my suspicion is that it would be simple for him to slip across the border to investigate any problems that cropped up here."

"Hans who?" Claire asked, startled.

"Wermager. You see, when the thefts occurred the government took steps to keep tabs on several international criminals who were suspected of being connected to the ring. Everybody stayed put minding their own business except for a man named Hans Wermager. He hopped a flight to Winnipeg from his home in the Grand Cayman islands. I've done business with him before, in Europe, and I'm certain he's one of the masterminds behind the ring. He's a dangerous man. Capable of anything. That's why I want you to keep your head low—"

She shook her head adamantly. "Dan, don't discourage me from accompanying you. You know how much this means to me."

Silence stretched between them. Claire found it hard to contain her thoughts. "This is nuts," she scoffed. "Washstands and stoneware crocks? What stupid things to be chasing after."

"Not so stupid. When you smuggle something valuable, you try to make it look as mundane as possible."

"But the last piece went out in a washstand. Why use crocks, too?"

"I don't know they'd pick crockery, but it would be awfully conspicuous to bring ten or twelve washstands over the border, Claire. People generally buy antiques one piece at a time, not in case lots." Dan began rocking slowly again. "I don't understand how they could get something into a crock to begin with."

"A false bottom, I'd assume. Probably cut the base off and replaced it with fiberglass with documents sealed inside of it."

"That would work?"

"Sure," Claire asserted. "It would conceal the document but wouldn't stand up to scrutiny. The bottom would be too lightweight, but they could disguise the texture with plaster, I suppose."

"So not knowing how to detect a false-bottomed crock, this Zendler scratched at the design and then probably examined it with a magnifying glass to see if the wing was painted above or below the glaze."

"Your theory makes sense, Garner," Claire exclaimed. "That would explain the magnifying glass Burt found lying on the floor by the case. Anyone familiar with stoneware would be able to tell at a glance if it was an underglaze or an overglaze on the pot, but an amateur might have trouble spotting it."

"So, our smugglers made a fake crock Redwing or something and used it to smuggle the papers out of the country. I'd guess that it's the Holloway letter in the crock. It's the most valuable document in the collection, the one most worth stealing."

"My God," Claire exclaimed suddenly. "I may have met the man on Sunday afternoon!"

"What do you mean?"

"A man came in looking for a two-gallon Redwing crock. He asked for one specifically."

"What did he look like?"

"He was tall with fairly long brown hair. There was gray in his hair, too. I'd guess he was about forty-five. Dark eyes and a hooked nose. I figured he was another antique dealer because of the way he was examining everything so closely.''

"That was Hans Wermager," Dan said, slapping his leg. "There's a warrant out for him for fraud, so it must be important if he entered this country personally. Damn! It's beginning to make sense."

Claire looked confused. "I don't understand... what makes sense?"

Dan smiled at her. "Zendler must have been trying to double-cross the ring. He's an insider, who tried to steal the goods he knew had been transported to Walter's shop before they were sent up to Winnipeg."

"How do you know he's one of them? Maybe he just caught wind of the ring's scheme, and decided to cash in himself?" she asked.

Dan shook his head. "The ring is too airtight, and Wermager would have sent a henchman to do what he's doing himself. No, Wermager is angry and came to solve the dilemma himself. He's looking for a man he employed."

"But this traitor, this Zendler, doesn't have the contraband. He's still looking for it himself."

"That's right, but his boss doesn't know that. Wermager has crossed the border to stalk his turncoat employee down and recover the goods. He thinks Zendler has the big prize, the million dollar Holloway letter."

Claire's reply was interrupted by an insistent rap on the door of the shop. She hopped down from the desktop to run lightly to it.

"Afternoon, Claire," Burt Peterson said, stepping inside and waiting while she pulled the door shut behind him. "We just got done talking to Mrs. Sanderson."

"Good. You were both out when we called," Claire told him as she led the way back to where Dan sat waiting by the counter. "I hope you don't mind that we went out ahead of you, but we couldn't wait."

"Actually, we do mind, honey." The big man watched Dan warily, a scowl growing on his face. "This is an official investigation, you know."

"Yes, of course. But since it involves my uncle, I didn't think it would hurt anything."

"I know. And I don't imagine it was your fault, Claire. It's good there wasn't any evidence to be disturbed." Burt unzipped his heavy jacket and pushed it back slightly, exposing the butt of his service revolver. "But from now on you'd do better to wait and let Uncle Burt do his job."

"What do you mean there wasn't any evidence?" Claire asked, ignoring his warning. "What about the crocks?" She leaned her hip against the counter, crossing her arms over her chest.

"Yes, they told us you two were interested in that pottery, and the scratches on them. Claire, those scratches could have happened any time."

"Then why were their houses broken into?" Dan broke his silence with a defiant question.

"Kids, most likely." His pointed reply was delivered in a hard tone as he stared into the seated man's eyes. "You know how they are, sometimes."

"Sure, I know how they are," Dan said blankly.

"But why would kids break into those homes?" Claire's voice was laden with disbelief. "And what about the man I fought with?"

"I'm sure he's connected in some way to the troubles here, but I can't see any connection to either the

Sanderson house or Albertson's farm. Sorry, Claire,
I'm sure you're excited about your theory, but it doesn't
hold water."

"My God!" Claire exclaimed, pushing herself away
from the counter to face the officer. "It all makes sense,
Burt! Why did he scratch those pots?"

"You've got no proof the crocks were scratched recently, Claire." The older man looked at her as he might
look at a confused child. "We've got to use some logic
when we check out the facts, honey."

"But this is logical!" she cried. "Once you see how
it all fits together, you'll see that it makes sense. I didn't
believe it at first, either, but there's no other way to look
at it. Especially when you know about the shop in
Winnipeg, and—"

"Forget it, Claire," Dan cut her off, sharply. "He's
written off the whole thing in his mind, and you aren't
going to change that block of stone to any other opinion."

"I don't need any noise from you, Garner!" Sheriff
Peterson wheeled on him, glowering. "Just because you
managed to twist some facts around to fit your argument doesn't make the argument right."

"Nor does it make it wrong."

"Well I know one set of facts that can't be twisted!"
Burt planted his fists atop his hips, pushing the jacket
back further from the black bulk of the gun. "There are
a few facts about you that could use some explaining."

"About me?" Dan's eyebrows went up over his
amused grin. "Did you get your information?"

"Oh yes, and there's more on the way, I'm sure."
Burt turned toward Claire suddenly. "Has your boy-

friend told you what he's been up to since they kicked him out of the navy?''

"He's not my boyfriend," Claire replied. An icy hand clutched at her heart as she faced the officer. Kicked out of the navy?

"Whatever he is, he hasn't been a good boy." He reached into the pocket of his jacket and withdrew a folded sheet of paper. "Did he tell you that he's been arrested three times for possession of stolen property and twice for illegal transportation of munitions?"

"Tell the truth, Dan," Claire insisted. "Don't waste everyone's time on this nonsense."

But Dan remained silent, calmly rocking the old oak chair with a smile stamped on his face.

"Or did he happen to mention that he's listed prominently in the records of several investigations into gun and drug running in south Florida. I think it's about time the town's prodigal son comes clean. Well, Garner?"

"Well, what?"

"What do you say about any of this?"

"I don't say anything about it," Dan told him, smiling slightly. "I haven't said anything to you yet, and I don't intend to start now."

"Come on, Dan, no more games." Claire was outraged by his continued silence. All he had to do was to explain things. After all, Burt Peterson wasn't an unreasonable man.

"I think the facts speak for themselves," Burt added. Then he turned back to Claire with a triumphant look on his face. "Dan Garner is just a plain, garden-variety thief."

"Say something, Dan." Claire glared down at him, her hands planted angrily on her slim hips.

But Dan only sat stoically silent, though he had stopped rocking. Finally he spoke. "I can't dispute facts, Claire. And my explanation would be nothing more than words at this point. But I could point out that our erstwhile officer doesn't have any convictions on his list of facts, nor will he find any."

"Is that true, Burt?"

"He's right. The bastard slipped out of all the charges. He's got the money for fancy legal help. Isn't that right, Garner? Money is a nice thing to have when you're in trouble, isn't it?"

"Damn right, Burt. It never hurts."

The two men stared at each other, Burt Peterson standing tall over the man seated below him. Antagonism sparked between them like an electrical current that seemed to hum in the silent room. Finally Burt shifted his weight toward Dan, drawing himself up taller.

"Lloyd Albertson said he saw a fancy car drive past his yard after his intruder left last night. It was a Mercedes, gray, like yours," he said. "Come on, Danny, let's go down to the office and see if we can come up with some kind of statement."

"Are you arresting him, Burt?" Claire demanded.

"No, but I'd strongly suggest that he come answer my questions."

"He doesn't have to go anywhere with you."

"That's all right, Claire. I don't mind having a friendly visit with good old Burt here." Dan stood, still smiling, and walked past the big man while Claire stood behind the counter livid with impotent rage.

"Tell him what's going on, Dan!" she exclaimed as the two men walked toward the door. "Say something!"

"I've got nothing to say at the moment." Dan grinned, taking his jacket from the rack by the door. "But I'd suggest that you check on Walter's suppliers—to confirm what we were talking about," he said cryptically. "I'll be back in a couple of minutes."

"Don't be so optimistic, Garner." Burt laughed, holding the door open. "Let's go."

The sheriff pulled the door shut behind them, cutting off the bitter wind that rustled through the shop. Claire stood for a moment staring at the door.

Chapter Six

"What were you doing out there, Danny?" Burt Peterson creaked back in the chair behind his desk and regarded Dan coldly.

"Don't I get a lawyer, Burt?"

"Do you need one?"

"I can't be too careful when I'm dealing with you, Burt." Dan sat quietly grinning, taunting the officer with his apparent lack of concern.

"Still as glib as ever, aren't you." Burt swiveled his chair to the side and stood. "I think your wisest move would be to get out of town, Danny. You generate trouble everywhere you go, and I just don't want trouble."

"Afraid you can't handle me this time, Burt?"

"Listen up, buster!" The officer leaned over his desk and glared at Dan. "Your papa isn't around to buy you out of everything, and Walter is in the hospital, so he can't run interference for you. And I'm not going up for re-election this time around, Danny, so it wouldn't matter what they said, anyway. You're on your own now. Handling you isn't something I'm concerned with," he said in a pinched, angry voice. He hitched back in his chair slightly and removed the gun from the holster riding his hip, placing the weapon on the desk before him. The threat hung heavily between them. "I can take care of a punk like you anytime. But I won't have you messing up Claire. You did the right thing once, Garner, you left her alone. You'd better be smart this time, too. Get out of town."

Dan forced a smile over the knot of angry muscles in his jaw.

"Claire is all grown up, Burt. She doesn't need any help from you."

"Shut up, Danny, and get out of my town."

"Or what, Sheriff?" Dan stood, glaring at him. He ignored the gun between them. "What are you going to do to me? I know your tricks, Burt. You can't bluff me out of town, and you can't prove I did anything, so what are you going to do to me? I'm not entirely helpless here."

"So you think." Burt laughed, a short explosion of amusement as he leaned back comfortably. "Keep believing that, Danny. See how far it gets you. Like you said, Claire is a big girl and she'll see through you eventually."

"And I see through you, Burt. You don't give a damn about Claire or her feelings. You're just looking out for number one, aren't you?"

"Get out of town, smart ass," Burt snarled. "We don't need you around here. I'm only doing what Walter would do if he was here. I'm just looking out for family."

"Sure you are, Uncle Burt," Dan said. "Sure you are."

OUTSIDE THE LARGE DISPLAY window of the antique store, the heavy gray clouds rushed across the sky in a race to bring snow to northern Minnesota, and the wind began to pick up in expectation of the coming precipitation. Winter was there to stay.

The door opened quickly at twelve-thirty, and Claire jumped up from where she'd been busy comparing inventory lists at the desk. "Dan?" she called, turning. But it was her cousin, Phillip, who approached her with his stocking cap clutched in one gloved hand.

"Just me," he said, shivering as he dropped his cap and gloves on the counter and unzipped his heavy coat. "Supposed to be a storm coming, but I think it's getting too cold to snow. How's everything shaping up in here? Has Burt come up with anything yet?"

"No, he doesn't have any idea what's going on," she said, her voice tinged with ironic anger. "And all he does is fight with Dan."

"So you and Danny were playing detective."

"One way or another, I'm going to find out who broke in here, Phillip. It's the least I can do for Walter. We thought we had a good lead, but I'm not so sure now. It looked like the thief was after a crock. But my count shows there was one already missing when the break-in occurred, so I'm not sure if our theory holds up anymore."

"How do you know what's missing?" Phillip asked.

"I compared Walter's purchasing book and last year's inventory with my latest accounting of the crocks. Walter bought several of varying sizes this year and even if you take into account the three crocks he sold recently—and the one shattered in the burglary attempt—we come up a crock short."

"What does Danny think?" Phillip's brow puckered in thought as he leaned one arm on the cash register and looked at her.

"He went off with Burt an hour ago. I'm expecting him back soon. Say, you know anyone named Jason?"

"Me? Why should I?" He came around to look at the book she held open on the counter. "Who's Jason?"

"He's down in the purchase book several times. Once this year and five times last year. From Minneapolis, apparently."

"Oh, sure, he sold some stuff up here," the lanky farmer said, pointing one thin finger at the lined book. "I remember Dad buying that hutch last fall. Never said the guy's name."

"It doesn't seem right for him to buy pieces from anyone in Minneapolis, does it?" Claire regarded the book thoughtfully. "Prices are higher in the city. But you can see that Walter didn't pay Minneapolis prices for any of the stuff. This Jason fellow took a bath on the transaction."

"Dad is a better businessman than we thought." Phillip laughed briefly but without smiling. "What's wrong with a hayseed merchant getting the best of some city-slicker?"

"Nothing, except that it makes no sense. You don't suppose Jason is a relative of someone local who died and left him the estate? That might explain why he sold pieces to Walter."

"It's been a pretty healthy year, Claire. Not many people kicking off lately. None with any kind of estate, anyway."

"I didn't think so."

"How come you were messing around with last year's books?" he asked, looking off toward the front door.

"I've had some time on my hands. And when I saw Jason written in for last month, I thought I'd take a look and see if he'd sold anything up here before. Strange stuff, too. He sold an antique hutch, two china dolls, a washstand, a phonograph and an old painting of some kind, among other stuff. That's an odd assortment."

"What did he sell to Dad last month?"

"A grandfather clock, a brass bed, three crocks and a doll, along with another washstand." A look of excitement passed over Claire's face as she thought about the transaction. "Is that the grandfather clock that's sitting upstairs?"

"No. That one was shipped out last week. The clock upstairs on the other hand is mine," he said somewhat proudly. "Walter got both clocks in a couple weeks ago, and I snatched the best up for Janet. She's always wanted a grandfather clock, and I thought it was about time I got her one for Christmas. We're hiding it up there till then."

"What happened to the other clock?"

"He sold it to some guy from Winnipeg a couple days later."

"That's a lovely present, Phil. I think you might actually be able to surprise her this year. Now, I wonder if any of those crocks Jason sent up were two-gallon Redwings."

"Didn't Dad write down the sizes?"

"Not in here. You know how he keeps books, Phillip."

"Yes, I sure do," he said with a laugh. "He's the one who taught me how to do it."

"You're not still worried about money, are you?"

"Not really. I just got done having a little talk at the bank. It looks like I've managed to pull ahead of the race, and if next year is at least average I'll be out of the woods."

"See? Things are looking up."

"Yes, after thirty-two years I've finally begun to develop a little horse sense. Of course, one hell of a good harvest didn't hurt at all."

"No, it never does."

"Well, I'd better get along." He zipped his coat and slipped his gloves back on, patting his hands together somewhat nervously. "I'll be ready to go to Grand Forks soon. I'll stop by for you."

"I'll be ready."

"Good." Slipping the woolen stocking cap over his head, he walked to the door. "Bye now."

"Goodbye, Phillip," Claire called as he walked out.

What if their sleuthing came to nothing? She'd already poked one hole in their theory by proving that a crock was indeed missing. What if there were more holes, and everyone's investigations came to nothing? What if Walter— No, don't think that. Claire felt certain that if they kept their minds on the clues, they'd be able to capture the man who had put her uncle in the hospital. They would capture all the men behind the crimes and Walter would recover, simply because that was the only outcome that Claire would accept.

She'd found another anomaly in those entries about Jason from Minneapolis which served to rebuild the theory. She noted that Walter had checked off each item on last year's inventory as sold. It was too bad she didn't have the receipt book to see who'd bought them. There was no way for them to know if any of Jason's merchandise was even still in the area.

"So you've come up with a new clue, have you?"

The sudden question burst from nowhere, sending Claire into a defensive spin away from where she'd been standing at the counter. Dan Garner was walking out from the back room.

"What are you— How did you get in?" she demanded, sudden anger boiling over.

"Walter should buy a better lock for the back door. Did I scare you?"

"You're damn right, you scared me! Why on earth did you come in like that?"

"I'm a sneak thief, remember? Just keeping in practice."

"Quit joking around."

"Okay." He walked up to her, sliding one hand along her arm. "There was no parking space out front, so I stuck my car out back. I stopped in to say goodbye."

Claire shrugged his hand away, turning her head to hide her smile. "Are you going someplace?" she asked.

"Minneapolis."

"When will you be back?" Sardonic humor lit her emerald eyes as she looked at him.

"Maybe I won't be back," he said seriously.

"That's about par for the course," she commented. They still had that score to settle. "When are you leaving?"

"An hour ago, if possible." He hopped up to sit on the desktop, watching her with eager eyes. "You and I have both found connections to the Twin Cities, and I'd best follow them up."

"You and I? You heard my conversation with Phillip?"

"Sure did. I was about to leap out and surprise you when I heard the cowbell clanking, and I didn't want to explain my foolish behavior to any more people than I absolutely had to."

"Okay," she said with an affectionate smile. "So, you know about this Jason fellow and his tie to the suspect shipment of goods. But there's no entry for Zendler, whom you mentioned before."

Dan shrugged. "Jason is probably a key suspect, but he's nothing more than a front for Zendler and the others. Which is why I have to go to Minneapolis."

"Why?"

"Because from Zendler's car registration I learned he lives in St. Louis Park, and my hunch is that Jason lives nearby. We need to get as much information about the ring as possible if we're to move ahead. I know that Zendler has returned home because I called his motel and learned he checked out at eight yesterday morning."

Claire stared at him, an idea coming to mind. "What kind of car was Zendler driving?"

"A dark brown Chevrolet sedan," Dan answered easily. "Why?"

"Because someone in a dark brown sedan was watching the shop on Sunday. And yesterday he was outside again parked across the street. I went out to confront him, and he took off like someone had lit a fire under him."

"Did you see him?"

"No, the sun was against me, but it must be the same man."

"Well, there you have it, then. He's got to be the man who clubbed Walter!" The determination lighting Dan's eyes radiated an aura of passion that flooded the room with its clear light. "We'll get him yet. That's why I have to go south, Claire. I booked a seat on a flight out of Grand Forks at five, so I've got to step on it." He swung his feet around and jumped down from the desk.

"I'm coming with you," she said decisively.

"Why?"

"Because Walter is my uncle, and I'm going to do what I can to help." A fierce light shone in her eyes as she spoke, allowing for no argument.

"I can't justify bringing you into contact with these people," Dan protested. "This is a high stakes deal, Claire, and Hans won't stop at anything to make his money. The more time that passes, the more likely Hans will close in on his targets, and we'll be within that range. You also have to remember that no one has found the missing crock yet, and that means that all three are quite desperate. There may be some cross fire among Jason, Zendler and Wermager."

"You've told me that before, Dan, but Hans—and the others—are already alert to my presence. I won't be in any less danger with you than I would be waiting here."

"Be reasonable, Claire—"

"No, Dan, you be reasonable." Claire spoke with passion. "You're going to St. Louis Park to find a man named David Zendler, or Jason or a Mr. Jason. And I'm quite able to fly to Minneapolis and do the same without you."

"Claire, I wouldn't advise—" Then he paused and allowed a smile to grow on his face. "All right, I'm not going to win this argument. Let's get a move on."

"All right. Give me time to throw some things together," she said. "I'll have to call Phillip and tell him I won't be visiting him today. And if we leave as soon as possible, we'll have time to visit Uncle Walter."

EVEN THE SIGHT OF THE hospital didn't seem so daunting now that they were taking positive action to find Walter's assailant, and Claire went into Walter's room in hopeful spirits.

"Will he come out of it soon, Doctor?" Claire stood at the foot of Walter's bed with Ted Kirshner, a pleasantly rotund man with half-glasses pushed up in his thatch of gray hair.

"He's begun coming around," Dr. Kirshner told her, watching the man in the bed breathing slowly and regularly. "He's showing increased reaction to external stimuli, for one thing. That's always a good sign."

"But that doesn't necessarily mean he'll be coming out of it soon, does it?" Dan stood by the head of the bed looking down at the unconscious man. "What are the odds?"

"Can't make odds on head injuries very well, young man," the doctor said. "All of our tests have shown normal brain activity, however. No flat lines in any area affecting either motor functions or sensory perception. Nothing to indicate anything but a full and complete recovery." Then Dr. Kirshner shrugged slightly, saying, "Of course, good test results don't always spell recovery. We don't know enough about the workings of the brain to be able to predict anything with total accuracy."

"But your opinion now is that he'll recover completely?" Claire asked with anxious hopefulness.

"That's my opinion, yes. There may be some slight impairment at first, but I'm fairly certain he'll be up to full steam in no time at all. What he's doing now is resting, that's all it is. You see, in a case like this a coma is the brain's way of healing itself. Damaged brain tissue, of course, can't be repaired or replaced, but by retreating into sleep the damage can be minimized. Much the same way as we would put a cast on a broken arm, the brain insulates itself from further shock by retreating behind the barrier of sleep. Unfortunately, much like a broken arm, you can't tell how successful the repairs have been until the cast comes off."

And Walter Hoffner did seem to be sleeping peacefully, his skin tone healthy and his breath coming with a natural rhythm. But as Claire stood looking down at her uncle and watching Daniel as he sat quietly beside the reclining man, she couldn't hold back the thought that a person might easily look just as healthy lying in state.

Don't worry, Walter, she thought with fierce determination. *We'll find out who did this to you and keep them from hurting others.*

Chapter Seven

Northwest Orient Airlines flight 237 took on passengers in Grand Forks at 5:10 p.m. and was airborne at 5:30. It landed in Fargo at 5:55 and spent half an hour on the ground as more passengers boarded. By 6:30 they were once again soaring up above the heavy overcast that had reduced the hard light of the winter sun to dingy gray. The passengers debarked at the Minneapolis-St. Paul International Airport at 7:45.

Dan spent most of the flight in a strangely uncommunicative mood, replying to questions when necessary, smiling when appropriate and generally going through the motions of companionship, but doing it all in a woodenly forced manner. Claire tried to coax the reason for his quiet mood out of him but had no success. At the St. Paul airport he used a key to open one of the lockers and take out a small package which he slipped into the pocket of his coat. She didn't question him about it for he was still acting quiet, remaining aloof until after they'd picked up their luggage and rented a car, finally breaking through with a genuine smile as they drove out of the Avis parking lot.

They drove through the city without talking, content to absorb the city sounds and sights at night as they acclimated themselves to the abrupt change from the level plains of northwestern Minnesota.

Over Claire's protests, Dan took them into the center of Minneapolis and checked into two rooms at the Hilton. "I'm not going to spend the night in some fleabag to save a couple bucks," Dan told her as they followed the bellman up with their bags. "I've been forced to spend too many nights in too many disgusting rooms to be satisfied with cheap accommodations when I've got a choice."

"Oh, I've got no objection to traveling first-class," Claire said. "What shall we do about dinner?" she asked, standing beside the bellman as he stopped outside room number 610.

"Let's get freshened up and I'll call for you at ten of nine." Dan picked up his bags and continued walking to 611. "Bring your appetite."

Claire changed into her wool skirt and angora sweater, and by the time they entered the Hilton restaurant, her appetite was well up to the coming task. A hostess escorted them to a table near the back, and moments later a waiter arrived to take their order from the bar.

"I still don't have any idea how to find your Jason outside of calling the antique stores in town and asking about him. But I don't want to risk alerting him if I can help it." Dan spoke quietly as he relaxed against his chair and interlaced his fingers over his stomach. "I hope David Zendler can provide some information on him."

"But if Zendler is the man who broke into the shop, we may not need to find Jason," Claire said.

"No, we still need Jason. We've got to tie everyone together in a concrete way. There's a chance Jason was used as a front just like they used Walter. All we know for certain is that Hans Wermager is a key figure in the international ring's setup. The rest is just conjecture until we get proof."

Their conversation halted when their drinks arrived and they ordered their meal, each quickly consulting the menu as though dinner were more a hindrance than an occasion they enjoyed. The formality of ordering finished, Dan picked up where they'd left off.

"They've picked up the trail in Europe now," Dan said. "I spoke to Washington last night, and they told me the route the washstand, the two crocks and a ceramic doll took after being shipped from Winnipeg. The curio shop is in Paris, but the goods come in from several European points—London, Berlin and Rome, chief among them."

"Why so many cities?" she asked.

"Because for an overseas shipment it would be helpful to have an extensive purchase record that will stand up to scrutiny at various customs inspections en route."

"And inspectors would be reluctant to risk damaging an antique with too strenuous an investigation." Claire spoke with a knowledge born from her own experience in transporting antiques. "Those antique dolls Walter got from Jason would work quite nicely for hiding something small."

"Were old dolls hollow?"

"I don't know what kind of doll it was. Walter only listed them as china dolls in the inventory book, so I couldn't be entirely sure what he meant. But it wouldn't be that hard to hide something inside a doll.''

"And there are no dogs trained to sniff out jewels," Dan commented.

"Right. It would be a hand search that would be their biggest concern." Claire leaned across the table in excitement. "You're right then, Dan. If they have enough documentation proving ownership, they'll waltz right through a hand search."

Claire was amazed the words came out, let alone made sense. The almost physical touch of his eyes brought the insistent hammering of yearning excitement to her heart. Her memories hadn't deceived her. He was as strong and capable as she'd remembered, as humorous and vulnerable. Her heart took up the old rhythm of her love for him as she sat so teasingly close. But the gulf of their lost years still stretched between them.

"So we still have a pretty theory but no proof about the crocks. They might have been sent along as window dressing, just something to confuse the issue."

"No, there must be something in them." Claire's voice showed a confidence that easily matched his own, and a victorious smile lit her face as she spoke. "How many items were stolen from the exhibit?"

"Six pieces in total," he said. "But only the dispatch has any major dollar value. It's insured for over one million. Of course that wouldn't begin to cover its historical value."

"Okay. Last month Jason sent a single shipment to Walter." Claire ticked off the items on her fingers as she spoke. "There was a brass bed, three crocks, a china doll, a washstand and a grandfather clock. That's seven things. How big were the items? Could they have hidden more than one thing in a piece like a two-gallon crock?''

"They were all documents—letters, field dispatches and notes. All small, easy to hide, and each was sealed in protective plastic wrapping. Some of them are fairly brittle, so they couldn't be folded.''

"Then they could have fit several things in one item,'' Claire said. "Maybe even all in one. In that case, the crocks might indeed be window dressing.''

But that didn't explain why the burglar was after the crock. The thought didn't need to be stated between them.

"Would Walter have bought crocks that had been tampered with?'' Dan watched her seriously, but his eyes suggested an interest in something other than smuggling. They danced over Claire's face, lingering on her lips, the curve of her throat, and her hand still touching his. "He checks things out, doesn't he?''

"As much as I hate to say it, Uncle Walter isn't the best antique dealer in the country. He may not have checked the goods too closely.''

"Until we know otherwise, we'll have to go on the assumption that all but one of the items Jason sent to Walter had contraband hidden on it.''

"They probably did. Why risk losing everything by putting them all in one thing?'' Claire sat up, an idea suddenly coming to mind. "Dan, we know that Jason sent three crocks to Walter last month, and that Walter sent a shipment with only two in it to Winnipeg. What if he should have really sent three, but somewhere along the way it got lost? Maybe that third crock from Jason is the one everyone's looking for?''

Dan smiled. "You may be right. But without the receipts book we'll never know to whom Walter mistakenly sold it. The point is that a crock is missing, whether it was in that last shipment of three, or among an earlier batch."

Claire settled back, her eyes dimming as his thumb stroked the delicate ridge of her knuckles to send a tingle through her. "Jason must have been using the shop for smuggling long before this."

"And probably working with Hans all along. It would make sense for them to make use of an existing conduit for the booty."

"All you need is proof that Zendler and Jason are part of the smuggling and you've sewn the whole thing up. You must be right about that Wermager fellow, too," she said. "He was probably in Garner Falls to find out what was going on at the shop. Zendler has to be double-crossing them."

"That's the only logical answer I can think of." Dan scowled. "We still need to find one more person in Garner Falls. I need one more."

Claire leaned back, disgusted with him. "Not that again, Dan! Who else could there be? Why can't Zendler have just set Walter up because the town is near the Canadian border?"

"Someone connected up your uncle with Jason, Claire," he said flatly. "There's still that connection to be made."

"You can't be serious!" Her fingers relaxed slightly, the warmth growing from his touch cooling in the icy hardness of his accusation.

"Has to be." He stretched his lower lip against his teeth, chewing it lightly. He was stubborn on this one.

"Hoffner's Antiques has always been a local operation. Think about it. Has Walter ever gone on a buying trip for that place?"

"No, not that I know of."

"I didn't think so. It's not so much a business for him as it is a place for his friends to drop in and chat and maybe get in a couple of hands of pinochle. He doesn't need any huge income out of the place, so why make trouble by looking for more stock? So the only way he would get in touch with Jason is through someone in town. And as you pointed out, this Jason fellow is selling his stuff far too cheaply. He had to have enlisted someone local to give Walter a plausible story that explained those remarkable cut rates."

"You're right," she sighed, admitting to one more strike against the town she'd once felt was picture perfect, one more blot on her memories. Claire looked sad for a moment. "I just wish we had that receipt book so we knew whom Walter sold that crock to."

"Zendler will tell us that. He has that book in his hot little hands. Chances are it wasn't someone local or there'd have been another break-in." Dan squeezed her hand tighter as an anxious frown darkened his features. "Since we're so far behind Zendler you may as well know, Claire, we may have lost that crock forever. And without other proof, it will be damn hard to pin the break-in on Zendler."

"We'll get proof," Claire declared, angered by the invasion of Garner Falls by cutthroats and international thieves.

"I'm sure we will...now that the two of us are working on this together. Two heads are better than one, as they say." He spoke low and in a comfortable tone, but his eyes sparkled with an excitement that didn't pretend to be caused by their quest.

Claire returned his loving gaze in kind, examining the creases the sun and wind had carved in his face. She liked what she saw and was no longer afraid to let her eyes admit it. And she liked being there with him. It was such a comfortable feeling; the touch of his warm, lightly callused hands on hers made her feel safe, almost exempt from the pains that life and love had already inflicted on her. Their common past and common goal created a new bond. It was a wondrous feeling to get such a compassionate glow from another human being's touch and the gentle consideration of his eyes. She'd gone so long without that spark of passion.

The arrival of the waiter with their meal interrupted her thoughts and cut off further discussion for the moment. It was only then that Claire remembered how hungry she had been. When they finished their meal, Dan brought them back to the matter at hand with a discussion of the next day's activities.

"Tomorrow in the safety of daylight we'll visit Mr. Zendler's apartment. We'll wait until then also because it's likelier that Zendler will be gone during the day, and we don't want to take any chances. If we look around, I'm sure we'll find something that will help us find Jason."

"And if we come up empty?"

"We wait for him to come home, which is not my preference."

"Why don't you call some of your men in since Zendler and Jason may be so dangerous?" Claire asked.

Dan looked serious a moment. "The back-up will be there if it turns too ugly, but right now we need to gather evidence as quietly as possible so we don't scare off the entire gang.''

"Will I ever learn the tricks of your trade?" she asked with teasing seriousness. "I might like doing under-cover work."

"So you bought my story, did you?"

"I guess I must have."

"What a guppy," he said, leaning closer over his coffee cup and speaking very softly. "I'm glad you were in town, Claire." One strong hand reached out to stroke the silken curve of her cheek, and follow it to the softly rounded point of her chin. "I still love you, Claire," he said.

"Please, stop it," she told him, feeling a blush rising in her cheeks. "I don't want another thing on my mind right now. I've got enough confusion."

"Am I confusing you?"

"Yes, I'm afraid you are." She reached up and cir-cled his wrist lightly with her fingers. "I've barely been divorced a year and here you come like a big question mark into my life. I'm not sure I'm ready for this yet."

For a moment their eyes remained locked. But she broke the contact by looking away in confusion. *Why can't this be simple?*

Dan shifted suddenly and Claire looked up, about to say something, anything, to change the subject when she saw that he was looking over her shoulder toward the bar. His expression was tense with anxious concen-tration.

"What's wrong?"

"Just a second," he whispered. Then he pushed his chair back and stood, moving swiftly around the table. "I'll be right back."

Claire turned and watched him stride toward the bar. A dark-haired man in a windbreaker was moving toward the exit. Dan hastened his steps, sliding his right hand beneath his sport jacket and back so the elbow stood out like a wing. Claire stood, moving a couple steps away from the table. She could see the man in the windbreaker stumble against a couple on their way out as Dan caught the collar of his jacket with his left hand and spun him up against the edge of the bar.

The man shoved Dan's hand away, saying something in anger. Dan replied, leaning against the shorter man and emphasizing his point with a sharp jab against the man's chest. Then he stepped back, his right hand still hidden beneath his jacket, and watched the other man scurry away.

Only after the man in the windbreaker was completely out of sight did Dan bring his empty hand out. He smoothed his jacket down. And when he looked up toward the balcony, his eyes were fierce and cold.

My God, Claire thought, *if looks could kill, I would have just witnessed a murder.*

"Moss Hunter." Dan identified the man before Claire could ask as he returned to his seat. "Hans Wermager's gofer. He's a petty thief, a leech, and he's not much by himself, but this probably means that Hans is definitely around."

"Is he dangerous?"

"Only if Hans tells him to be." He sipped his coffee, a worried look creasing his brow.

"Are he and Hans the type of men you're accustomed to doing business with?"

"Yes, a real fun crowd."

"I don't know how you can stand it," she said earnestly. "But, for that matter, if you've dealt with them before, why haven't they been arrested?"

"No concrete evidence. What I know and what I can prove are two separate things." Dan sipped his cooling coffee, a look of frustration crossing the rugged plane of his face. "Wermager seems to have a sixth sense working to snoop out listening devices, cameras, or any other traps I've tried to lay over the years. He just refuses to incriminate himself anywhere that I might be able to record it, and since he usually plays from behind the scenes, it's impossible to catch him in the act."

"He's not behind the scenes this time."

"No, he's not. And this may be the only chance I get to catch him red-handed."

"And we're going to do just that, Dan," Claire said, forcefully.

"Yes, I think that this time we are." He stood, taking the check from the small tray by his cup. "Let's go. Tomorrow's going to be a long day."

"He's seen us together now." Claire stood beside him as he dropped several bills on the tray beneath the dinner check. "Do you think Moss Hunter knows who I am?"

"If his boss does, he does," Dan said, taking her arm within the crook of his own and grasping her hand.

He escorted her out of the restaurant calmly, but his eyes were in constant motion, searching the people at the bar and the few couples standing outside. No one spoke to them or seemed to notice their passage, but Claire felt as though she was walking on hot coals. In the elevator, Dan pushed the button for the fifth floor, one floor below their rooms.

"You don't mind walking up a flight, do you?"

"That's a bit melodramatic," Claire said, smiling, though she was glad to take the precaution.

"Cops and robbers," he said, holding the door to the stairs open for her. "And I'm going to do a quick check of your room before you turn in, too. I'm not taking any chances with your safety." He opened the door to the sixth floor, looking through before allowing her to pass. "Come on, give me your key."

She handed him her room key, leaning against the wall as he opened the door and entered. A minute later, he came out, grinning.

"All clear," he said holding the key out. "Our hotel prides itself on maintaining rooms clear of booby traps or lurking prowlers. Sleep tight."

"Thanks, Dan."

As she passed him in the doorway he stopped her with one hand and drew her into his embrace, capturing her lips with his. His strong arms slipped confidently around her shoulders to hold her close against his broad chest. She responded to the kiss with an urgency equal to his, savoring the long-absent taste of his lips, the well-remembered pressure of his arms encircling her with warm strength. She held him with an impulsive need to capture every sensation she could while their embrace lasted.

If it could only last forever. If she could only trust her feelings for this man. She had yet to get his explanation for what happened years ago.

But it was over all too soon. He stepped back, his eyes smoldering with unfulfilled desire. He trailed his hands over her shoulders as though unwilling to lose contact with her until absolutely necessary.

"Good night, Claire." His voice was smooth with sensual heat to match his eyes, the tone conveying everything his words left unsaid.

"Good night."

Claire slipped through the door quickly, escaping his magnetic presence before she could give in to the impulse to invite him in.

Chapter Eight

At nine, Wednesday morning, they left the downtown area and headed west under a cloudless sky, a dazzling dome of blue above them. The radio weather forecaster had announced the approach of a winter storm, and Claire had worn her down coat and heaviest wool slacks in preparation, but the temperature was in the mid-thirties and there wasn't a hint of inclement weather in the breeze that circulated through the city.

"When we get there, we'll park down the street and walk back to the apartment and find a way in," Dan told her as they crossed into St. Louis Park. "I don't want anyone to get a look at the license on the car. We'll be noticeable enough no matter how we approach the place, but we're less likely to cause suspicion if we walk right on in like we're supposed to be there."

They were driving through a quiet residential neighborhood. The houses were lined up in pristine rows, the light dusting of snow scraped carefully away from the driveways and sidewalks.

"We should talk to his neighbors about him," Claire suggested.

"No, we'll be ahead of the game by frisking his apartment in private rather than announcing ourselves."

Breaking in? Claire hadn't considered the possibility and was as much as shocked by his suggestion as she was by her naiveté in not thinking of it. "What if we're caught?"

"Who's going to catch us? Mr. Zendler? He won't press charges. I'm afraid you'll have to trust the instincts of a housebreaker on this one, Claire."

A small smile played across his lips as he drove, revealing his determination. "This is the address I got," Dan told her as they drove through an older section of the city.

The neighborhood had declined into disrepair, the blocks filled with private homes converted to apartments, each with their own collection of cars taking up the driveways and yards. Morning light improved the fading paint on the houses but couldn't cover the decrepit look of the neighborhood, especially in contrast to the well kept, prosperous suburb they'd just passed through. Dan slowed the car by a two-story house composed of a series of additions to the original structure that had been added until the design of the house was totally lost. It had apparently been divided into three apartments with one on each of the three floors.

"He's listed for apartment number one, which I would assume is on the top floor. I hope it is, anyway, since there's an enclosed stairway running up the outside that will keep us under cover. The door at the foot is most likely unlocked, so we'll just go up and pick the lock on the apartment. Once we're in the stairway, we'll be all right."

"I don't like doing this," she admitted, watching the house with a wary eye as they passed. "It puts us right down to his level."

"Sure, but that's where we have to go to catch him."

He drove slowly down the street and parked a block away from the house. There were very few cars parked on the street.

"What if it's the wrong guy?" Claire asked.

"There won't be anyone there to know. Come on, let's get this over with."

He threw his door open and stepped out, the light wind ruffling his thatch of dark hair. Claire joined him slowly, pulling her winter jacket closed and carrying her gloves. He walked around the car, offering her his hand.

"Just walk up casually," Dan cautioned as they turned at the sidewalk approaching the house. "Don't look around too much or appear in any way curious about the place. You want anyone who might see us to think that, for whatever reason, we're supposed to be here."

The sidewalk circled the house and they followed it around to the stairway enclosure tacked on to the side of the building. As he'd said, the outer door was open, and the mail slot beside it was labeled "D. Zendler," confirming that he occupied the top level.

"That was the hard part," Dan said, relief in his voice as he closed the outer door behind them. "Up we go."

"Let's get this over with," she said, following him. She felt a rush of nervous fear engulf her, making her aware of every small creak of the steps, every shift in the wind outside.

Dan knocked on the door and waited, then he knocked again. Claire said nothing but stood close to him, and he slipped his arm around her shoulder as they waited for the answer that didn't come. After a moment he released her with a slight squeeze of her shoulder and tried the doorknob. It was locked.

"Just another minute," he said, unbuttoning his pea jacket.

Claire didn't think she could stand to wait another minute as he removed a flat leather case from his breast pocket and leaned over the knob. Someone could come at any time—a nosy neighbor, a friend coming to call, anyone. All it took was one person who knew they had no business there and one call to the police, and their investigation would be abruptly over.

But that was a known consequence. What about the unknown that lurked inside the apartment? Someone could be waiting, armed and ready for them. She didn't know if she wanted him to hurry and get the door open or be thwarted by the lock.

Claire couldn't see past his shoulder as he worked on the knob, but only seconds after he'd begun the door swung open. He straightened up, slipping a length of thin wire back into the leather case. He stepped into the apartment cautiously, glanced around and then motioned for her to enter.

Claire's heart pounded as she walked through the doorway into the dim interior. She was his accomplice in a criminal act, and no matter what her motives, she'd joined him of her own free will and would be fully liable if they were caught. She could only hope to God that they weren't.

The main room was large and sparsely furnished but cluttered with the mementoes of a man living alone. To her right as she stood just inside the door, she noticed a bookcase holding a small assembly of paperback books and some videotapes. A fat reclining chair and a brass floor lamp occupied the corner beyond the bookcase with several magazines lying scattered on the floor beside it. There was a worn, sagging couch with a scuffed coffee table in front of it sitting below the window. The television stood on a stand in the other corner, a video-cassette recorder on the shelf below it. A ladder-back chair and end table made up the rest of the living-room furniture. Odds and ends, other people's discarded furnishings.

To her left was a bentwood rocker and an end table that matched the first. An imitation wood kitchen table set with four vinyl-covered chairs stood cluttered with dirty dishes and opened mail. A small kitchen area had been built into the corner. Dirty dishes filled the sink.

Between the kitchen and living room a short hall led back to four closed doors, three of them probably opening onto two bedrooms and the bathroom while the fourth, fitted with a narrower frame, obviously led into a linen closet.

When Dan was certain they were alone, he turned to Claire.

"Start here by the door and work around to the right. I'll go left. You know what to look for. And wear your gloves." He slipped on his own leather gloves as he spoke.

"Do you do this often?" she said, trying to tease away her own nervousness. Her hands shook as she pulled on her knit driving gloves.

"I believe I'll stand on my Fifth Amendment rights on that one," he said. Then he turned on a lamp and began sorting through a pile of magazines and miscellaneous papers on the table by the rocking chair.

"I hope they'll believe that you forced me to do this after the neighbors call the cops and they haul us away in handcuffs," Claire said, turning her attention to the bookcase. "I'm just an innocent girl who's been led astray by an old neighbor who said he was a G-man."

Humor was the best antidote for sheer terror, she decided. She sorted through the books quickly, looking for any papers standing between the volumes. Nothing. Nor was there anything between the videotapes on the shelf.

"They'll never buy it," Dan said, picking up her taunt. He abandoned the table by the rocking chair and moved to the kitchen set. "You'd better plead insanity."

"That's certainly closer to the truth." Claire got down on her hands and knees and peered beneath the bookcase. There was nothing but dust between the bottom shelf and the flattened weave of the carpet. "I have to be absolutely out of my mind to be doing this. Why couldn't we talk to the police?" She found nothing behind the bookcase, either.

"I don't like being laughed at," he said.

"So it's better to break into the apartment of some poor slob and skulk around like some criminal until your guys eventually pick him up?" She looked behind the recliner and then sat and picked up the magazines to sort through them. "He's going to know we've been here."

"As long as he doesn't know who's been here it won't matter."

"Here we go." Claire dropped the magazines back to the floor and hurried over to him holding a green slip of paper that she'd found lying between magazines.

"So he works for Delta Security in St. Paul." Dan accepted the paper. It was the stub of a paycheck made out to David Zendler in the amount of $630. "That's the outfit that handles security for the Walker Art Center."

"Looks like our boy has been doing some overtime," Claire said. "If you want to steal something, it doesn't hurt to have the guard on your side."

"He's our man, all right. I suspect if we look far enough into his background, we'll find he's moved around a lot from museum to museum, performing the same function for the ring. That way Wermager and his cronies don't have to retrain or bribe a willing or not-so-willing accomplice."

Claire looked around the room with disapproval. "That would explain this mismatched furniture."

"Yep," Dan said. "I suspect our fellow wanted to finally settle down, which would explain why he decided to turn on his organization and earmark the biggest prize for himself. Too bad he didn't know into which crock the antique dealer put the contraband; it would've saved time, and maybe Walter's head."

Claire put the pay stub on the table and went back to the couch and looked under the cushions. "I'd hate to be doing this for nothing. Doesn't Mr. Zendler ever dust or vacuum?"

"Bachelors live like pigs hoping to convince some woman that they need looking after. Didn't you know that?" He was busy looking through the cupboards in the tiny kitchen area.

"I'd hate to see your apartment," she called, leaning over the couch to scout the floor behind it, and trying to recover her humor.

"I don't have an apartment."

"Come on now," she said in disbelief. "You don't expect me to believe that, do you? Where do you keep your things?"

"Everything I need is in the trunk of my car." He came out of the kitchen and looked behind the television. "And everything I want to keep is stashed in a closet at my grandfather's house. I should call it my house now, since he willed it to me, but I can't get used to the idea. I never use the place."

"That's no way to live." Claire straightened up and faced him. "You've got to have someplace to call home."

"The house wouldn't be much of a home if I was living there by myself," he said. "I have no use for it unless I've got someone to share it with me."

"I think you'd better keep your mind on business, Dan."

"Okay. Try the baseboards," he told her.

"What?"

"You can cut a piece of baseboard loose and make a hollow space behind it to hide things." He went behind the wooden chair and kicked the board lightly, then moved around behind the television and tried again. "This guy is a security guard, so we should assume he knows something about the business. Baseboards make pretty good little safes.''

Claire went back to the door and kicked the baseboard beside the bookcase. It sounded solid enough to her.

Dan pulled the couch away from the wall and walked along kicking the baseboards, moving around behind the recliner and up to meet her at the bookcase.

"Nothing," he told her.

"Hold on," she said, walking around him toward the kitchen. "There's a little trick I've used before that he might be partial to."

"What are you talking about?" he asked, following her.

She threw open the door of the refrigerator and looked in, finally reaching behind a six-pack of beer to withdraw a jar of mayonnaise. "Shall we make some lunch while we're here?" she asked, unscrewing the lid and holding the jar out to him.

"It's full of money."

"See what he did?" Claire tilted the jar, showing him the side. "It's a simple trick if you have anything valuable you'd like to hide. You pour a bit of slightly off-white paint into an empty mayonnaise jar and swirl it around until you've coated the sides. Let it dry and you've got a nifty little hiding place. Just pop your valuables inside and stick it in the back of the fridge. The only thing to give it away is that real mayonnaise wouldn't normally fill the jar so evenly. After all, you don't put it into the refrigerator until after you've used some of it."

She took off one glove, reached into the jar and pulled out a loose stack of bills. Then she put the glove back on and pushed a cup and saucer back on the table to make room to lay them out.

"Mr. Zendler had good cause to hide this," Dan said, examining one of the bills. "Let's see how many there are."

"It's a thousand-dollar bill," she said, tensing a bill between her hands. "I think we're right about this guy."

"Of course we are. There are twenty-five of them." Dan looked at her significantly. "And the serial numbers appear to be in sequence."

"In sequence? You'd have to draw them directly from the bank to get them all in order." Excitement gripped her as she stared back into his laughing eyes.

"It means he hasn't been saving these bills up over years of careful living. He got them all at one time."

"As a payoff."

"You read my mind."

"Let's check the bedrooms," Claire said. She gave him back the bill and turned toward the hall.

"You're certainly getting into the spirit of things now," Dan said as he put the money in the jar and put it back into the refrigerator. "We still need an address for Jason."

"And we need a receipt book." Claire opened the bedroom door on the left, revealing an unmade bed and scattered clothing.

She went to the dresser first, searching quickly through the clothing in the drawers. The bottom drawer contained several photograph albums and personal papers, which she hurriedly rifled through. It was nothing but old high school papers and family pictures. She didn't know which of the several boys pictured was

David Zendler, but he appeared to have come from a large and happy family.

She could hear Dan enter the other bedroom as she left the dresser and crouched to look beneath the bed. Nothing.

"Find anything?" Dan called.

"Nothing yet."

Claire opened the closet door, looking directly up at the spine of a red ledger book on the closet shelf. "Receipts," it said in gilded block letters. As she swung the door fully open, she felt something brush her ankle, and looked down at her feet. A hand lay beside her left foot, the fingers curled up slightly, and a shiver climbed up her spine. Her eyes followed the arm into the closet to meet the eyes staring up from the floor, wide and empty and as expressionless as two wet stones.

His mouth was slack, the lips bloodied. His other hand lay limp across his chest, his legs bunched up and twisted to fit into the closet. And there was blood on his chest and covering the closet floor and shoes he'd been laid on top of.

Claire stood staring down for a second, seeing everything and nothing as a grayness crept into the edges of her vision. Her lungs seemed to contract, squeezing out the vital oxygen as sweat gathered at her temples and her heart hammered against her ribs. Then she suddenly found the strength to move and jumped back from the outstretched arm, away from the sightless eyes.

"Dan." She called softly first, then managed to draw in enough breath to shout his name. "Dan!"

"Find something?" His voice seemed so far away.

"Come here!"

Sudden nausea swept over her, and she staggered through the door and into the bathroom where she clutched the edges of the washbasin tightly. She stared into the mirror of the medicine cabinet and fought the swelling sickness. Her face in the mirror was pale and drawn, looking years older, but it was alive and she stared at it hoping to wipe away the sight of the man's cold, dead eyes.

"What happened?" Dan stood in the doorway, then entered to grasp her shoulders, concern clouding his eyes.

"The bedroom closet," she said. "I...I found him."

"What?"

"Zendler. Look in the closet!" She shrugged off his hand, then turned on the cold water tap and tore off her gloves to bring the water up against her hot cheeks. "Oh, God, I found him," she murmured, closing her eyes against her fear.

Dan left her side to see what she had seen.

The quest had been changed and her triumph over finding the book was soured to grim determination that they achieve their goal as quickly as possible. Dan's warnings about the stakes the opposition was playing for had become painfully clear.

"Go wait in the living room." Dan returned, standing slightly behind her and looking into her eyes in the mirror. "We'll be done in a couple of minutes."

"Now we have to call the police," she said feebly, panting. "We have to report that."

"Of course, but not from here." Dan's face was grim and pale, and for a moment it appeared to Claire that his eyes were as empty as those in the closet. "He's been dead awhile. Put your gloves on and get out of here. And take the receipt book.''

Claire picked up her gloves from the edge of the basin and put them on. It helped to have something to do, even a small thing like putting on her gloves. She took the red book from Dan as he slipped in front of her at the basin. He was holding something else in his other gloved hand.

"What is that?" She looked past his arm at the object in his hand. It was a man's wallet, bloodied on one edge. "My God, Dan, you didn't go through his pockets!"

"Only one pocket," he said tensely. "Wait for me in the living room."

But she stayed at his side, watching as he looked briefly at the money in the long slot and then slipped out a stack of cards from a leather pocket sewn into the double-folded wallet. He sorted through the cards carefully, slowed by his gloved fingers, then pulled out a business card and held it up.

"There you go," he whispered.

The card was elegantly embossed with script lettering. It said, *Jason's Antiques and Artworks, Minneapolis. Harold Jason, Proprietor.* It listed no address but did give a telephone number. Perhaps more significantly, someone had scribbled something on the back of the card. *P.J. Ceramics.*

David Zendler had provided a clue in death that he might have denied them in life.

Chapter Nine

They stopped at a pay phone in the parking lot of a 7 Eleven store, and Dan slipped into the booth and closed the door. After hanging up the phone, he paged through the phone book chained to the metal table inside. A few minutes later, he got back behind the wheel and slammed the door.

"That takes care of David Zendler," he said. "I called anonymously and the police will send a unit to investigate." He fished a cigarette from his pocket and lit it, blowing out a harsh cloud forcefully. "Damn these things!" He rolled down his window and threw the cigarette out. "Did you look through the receipt book?"

"Yes," she said tensely, as she tapped the book on one knee. "There's nothing here to account for the missing crock."

"Then that means it was definitely stolen, and probably by Zendler. So, whoever got Zendler got the crock as well. Let's go find Mr. Jason," he said.

"Where is his shop?"

"I found a listing in the phone book. It's on Lake Street above Lake Calhoun." He put the car into gear and moved them out of the parking lot and into the traffic going south toward Minneapolis. "I also found a listing for P.J. Ceramics in Apple Valley."

"Good, then if we come up empty with Jason, we've got something to fall back on," Claire said. She spoke slowly, her lips feeling thick and numb. She fought to suppress the constant shivering cold she felt within her. "If they have anything to do with the attack on Walter, I'm sure we'll turn up something." Her own voice sounded distant, hollow.

"Are you all right?" he asked, as they let the flow of automobiles move them along. He placed his hand lightly on her knee. It felt like the only spot of warmth on her entire body, and Claire took it in hers.

"I feel cold," she said. "Shock, I guess."

"This is serious business." The muscles in his jaw tensed as he spoke, standing out in cords beneath his skin. "The attack on your uncle was probably done out of fright. But this was murder."

"Was he shot?" She had to know but didn't want to know; the last thing she wanted was more details.

"No, a single knife wound, but I couldn't say much else about it. I don't know much about those things."

"I would have thought you knew everything there was to know," Claire snapped, dropping his hand as she stared out the window beside her. "It's all part of your job isn't it?"

"I didn't put that body in the closet, Claire." Dan spoke slowly, his voice low and soft with patient compassion. "And I'm not accustomed to finding bodies in closets, either. It was a shock to me, too."

"But you didn't hesitate to search through his pockets, did you?"

"No, I didn't. And now we know where to find Jason."

Claire felt a rush of inarticulate anger and could have struck him. She was so desperate for something that would take the sour feeling of helplessness away from her that she was ready to strike out against anyone who offered themselves as a target. Humor had long ago fled as a defense mechanism. But Dan wasn't her enemy, and he didn't kill David Zendler, and her anger was only her frustrated reply to the seeming futility of trying to find a solution to the mystery. At that moment everything seemed futile.

"I didn't mean to snap at you," she said, reaching out to slide the tips of her fingers slowly down the heavy fabric of his pea coat.

"I know. Don't worry about it." He smiled, keeping his eyes on the highway. He turned onto Minnetonka Boulevard and drove east.

"Our sneak thief and assaulter is dead now, isn't he?"

"Yeah, and it's a whole new ball game. Now, instead of trying to figure out what happened after the incident at Walter's shop, we've got to go at it from the supply end of the equation. Harold Jason was associated with both your uncle and the man who put him in the hospital, so he's the man to see."

"And he may be the man who killed Zendler, not Hans Wermager."

"That's just one of the things we'll have to find out."

They found the antique store in a modest building facing the frozen expanse of the city-bound lake across the busy street. But it didn't seem that they were destined to find out anything that afternoon, for the shop was closed.

"Damn!" Dan thrust his hands into the pockets of his jacket and kicked the base of the door lightly. "I can't sneak us into this one, I'm afraid. Too many people around this part of town."

"Good. I don't need anymore surprises today." She stood by one of the long windows flanking the door and peered through the glass. "Can't see much inside," she said.

"Jason's private address wasn't listed in the phone book." Dan joined her, leaning against the window frame with his collar turned up against the wind off the lake. "We'll have to get his address someplace."

Dan pushed himself away from the wall, waiting while Claire tried again to see something in the dark shop. Beyond the display of art deco pieces in the window there was nothing to see. Everything was black inside. She turned away and joined Dan.

"We will get everything sorted out, you know," Dan said. He held out his hand to her, looking intensely into her eyes. "It's only a matter of making the right connections."

"And avoiding the wrong ones," she said, thinking of David Zendler who'd obviously made the wrong connection. She took his hand in hers, savoring the warmth and strength of it, needing its support, and they walked along the line of stores together.

"Shall we go find P.J. Ceramics?" Dan asked, watching a blue Mustang that had pulled up to park at the curb across the busy street. The occupant remained inside the idling car.

"Yes, that's our only lead so far." Claire couldn't help but notice the furtive haste with which he walked them to the car. She felt she was being left in the dark again, but what wasn't he telling her?

APPLE VALLEY LAY SOUTH of the city. The home of the Minnesota Zoological Gardens, it as only a half hour by car. It took another half hour for them to find the address tucked away on the edge of a quiet neighborhood and hidden behind a neatly trimmed hedgerow. Dan stopped the car on the street and kept the motor running. P.J. Ceramics had to be inside, though no outside sign advertised the business.

"Okay, Claire, here's where your expertise comes into play." He shifted in the seat to face her, speaking quickly. "You're the one who knows everything about pottery, so I'll stay with the car."

"But Dan, I'm not sure I know what to ask," she protested.

"Of course you do. You're here to buy some stoneware. Find out what you can. If this potter is involved, we'll need to establish a complete line of evidence to set up an airtight case."

"I'll have to find some way to find out if there's a connection to Jason. How do you suggest I go about doing that?"

"You'll think of something. This will be your field test at the Dan Garner school for spies."

Claire got out and walked around the hedge, closing her coat against the chilly wind. A drift of sun-crusted snow lay against the front of a modest ranch house hidden behind the pines. Claire mounted the steps and pushed the doorbell button on the frame of the door.

A woman in blue jeans and a University of Minnesota sweatshirt, with long blond hair fixed in a ponytail opened the door after the second ring. She was about Claire's height, though a bit heavier, and she squinted against the afternoon sun as she opened the storm door to greet her visitor.

"Yes?" Her voice was a feathery wisp of sound.

"Is this P.J. Ceramics?"

"Used to be, till my divorce changed my initials," the woman said, laughing. "But this is the place. I'm Patty Sloan."

"Good. I'm looking to purchase some clay pieces," Claire began, making up her story as she went along. "Stoneware, actually. You see, I'm opening a restaurant and would like to decorate in a rural motif. Spinning wheels and crocks, checked tablecloths and things like that. I was told that you make stoneware."

"That would depend on what you're looking for," she answered. Then she pulled the door further open and stood back. "Come on in, it's a bit chilly to talk business on the steps."

"Thank you." Claire entered directly into the living room from the front door. It was a long, narrow room decorated with modern efficiency and an emphasis on metal and glass materials. What pottery there was was confined to a couple of strictly functional planters and vases.

"Sit down. Would you like some coffee?" Patty Sloan stood indecisively by the kitchen doorway.

"No, thank you."

"Good." The woman laughed. "Because I don't have any made. Please sit down."

"Thank you." She sat on one end of the low couch. "You have a lovely home, Mrs. Sloan, though I expected you to have more ceramics than you do."

"Oh, my house used to look like a display room." The woman laughed. "But I got so tired of looking at clay every time I turned around that I could have screamed. I've moved all my pieces out to my workshop in the garage."

"I hadn't thought about that," Claire said, smiling in return. Then, speaking on sudden inspiration, she said, "A Mr. Jason said you might be able to provide us with some crockery. We'd like to recreate the style of some of the older crockery pieces. The old Redwing and Union Stoneware styles. That's the look I'd like for my restaurant."

"Harry recommended me?" Patty Sloan threw her head back in a surprised laugh as she sat opposite Claire on a bent-steel rocking chair, crossing one leg up beneath her. "I guess there's a first time for everything. He must have been in a magnanimous mood. Sure, I could throw some clay for you. Of course the styling is simple enough to copy, but I'd be using different clay. No one who's seen the original pieces would be fooled."

"Why is it so funny that he'd recommend your work?" Claire was perplexed by her reaction.

"I was married to him once upon a time," the woman admitted. "It wasn't an entirely friendly split, and I can only fall back on youthful exuberance as an excuse for ever saying 'I do' in the first place. He hasn't been trying to pass off any of my old crocks as antiques has he?"

"Your old crocks?"

"Yes, I did a batch of two-gallon crocks in the old Redwing style a couple years back. Some of them were split on the bottom, and I gave three to him. They weren't any good."

"No, he wasn't trying to sell them. Why do you ask?"

"I wouldn't put it past him to paint a logo on it and try to pass it off as the real thing," the woman said. "Probably would have if there was any real money to be made from antique crocks."

"Maybe I should think twice before buying from him, then." Claire stood. "He's holding several pieces of furniture for me. You might be able to help me there. I was supposed to pick up a hutch at his home today, but the shop was closed when I stopped by. Do you know where I might find him?"

"I don't keep in very close touch with Harry these days." The woman stood with her, a thoughtful frown creasing her features. "It isn't like him to close up shop like that on a weekday, though. He's probably home with the flu."

"Do you have his address?" Claire walked toward the door, speaking casually. "I'd like to buy that hutch before I leave town this afternoon."

"Sure, I can give you his address. It's the least I can do in exchange for his recommendation. He lives in Edina."

Patty turned and walked into the kitchen, returning a moment later with a slip of paper in her hand. "Here," she said. "Be sure to get a second opinion on anything you buy from him."

"Are you really suggesting that he'd forge antiques?" Claire took the paper with an address in Edina written on it.

"I'm not suggesting anything—I'm telling you. Good luck."

The woman opened the door, and Claire stepped back out to the chill December afternoon.

"Thank you for everything." Claire turned back toward the door. "When I've decided how much crockery I'll need for the store, I'll give you a call."

"I'm usually here," she replied. "Stop by any time."

"I will." Claire walked down the steps and past the hedge to where Dan was waiting in the idling car.

"Get in. Quick!" Dan spoke to her with terse command in his voice when she opened the car door, and he popped the car into gear and moved away from the curb quickly as soon as she'd slammed it shut behind her. "We've got company."

"What?"

"Blue Mustang behind us." Dan twisted the wheel hard at the first corner, accelerating into the turn. "He drove past twice while you were inside and then gave it up and parked down the block. He's following now."

"Who is it?" The goal of their quest seemed unimportant now that Claire knew she and Dan were the object of someone else's mission. She turned in the seat, looking through the back window of their rented sedan. The blue car was turning the corner behind them and speeding up to stay on their tail.

"I couldn't see who was driving. Someone is getting nervous." He took them around another corner, joining the swelling traffic on a main avenue. "He knows we've spotted him, but he hasn't dropped back," he said, thoughtfully.

"Does that mean something?" Claire turned to him, looking away from the car pursuing them. "I mean, he can't be dangerous, can he?"

"No. Not in public, anyway. But he must think of himself as dangerous if he's willing to continue once he's blown his cover." Dan piloted the car onto the highway heading north into the city, their rented Ford vibrating as it reached highway speed. "And we're sure not going to lose him in this car. Where the hell is rush hour traffic when you need it?"

"What are we going to do?"

"We'll get back into city traffic and ditch him somehow. I just wish we could find out who he is."

"It must be Moss Hunter, mustn't it?" Claire glanced cautiously over her shoulder at the blue Mustang following them in the thin traffic.

"Maybe, but there might be more players in this game than we realize." Dan's eyes narrowed against the winter sun as he looked from the road to the rearview mirror and back to the road.

A black limousine pulled onto the highway ahead of them as they approached the overpass where the roadway crossed Cliff Road. It moved sedately, growing closer rapidly as Dan continued driving in excess of sixty miles an hour with the Mustang holding its distance behind them.

"The last thing I need now is a Sunday driver," Dan mumbled, directing the car into the passing lane.

Claire watched the long black car nervously as they closed the gap between them. It was a Lincoln with a New York license plate and dark tinted windows. They were beginning to pass it when she saw the rear window sliding down as the car seemed to accelerate to keep pace with them. A dark object slipped through the window just as they pulled abreast of the car.

"Dan!" Claire ducked forward without thought even as she shouted. "Faster!" was all she could think to say.

Even as she spoke, he jammed his foot hard on the gas pedal, and their car was suddenly filled with shattered glass. It was over as soon as it began, and they were flying down the highway ahead of the black limo as the explosive echo of two shotgun blasts filled Claire's head. She stared in horror at the destruction brought about in two short seconds. They'd shot out the rear window and both of the side windows in back, showering Claire and Dan with glass, but hadn't fired in time to hit the front seat.

They rocketed past several other cars on the highway, but the limo and the blue Mustang stayed with them, drawing closer. Finally, the black Lincoln moved into the passing lane not more than ten feet behind them. Dan swerved to cut them off, and they countered his move with a shift to the right.

"What are we going to do?" Claire shouted over the rush of air streaming through the destroyed rear windows.

"Run like hell!" Dan shouted with a short laugh. The light of anger flashed in his eyes. He passed a station wagon with the limo in hot pursuit and began evasive maneuvers again. "This makes absolutely no sense at all!"

"That doesn't make me feel any better," she shouted, leaning closer to his ear.

"We'll stay on the highway till we're well within the city. It should be safe by then. I hope they don't know where we're staying." Dan watched the rearview closely, and Claire followed his gaze to watch the sinister vehicle in their wake.

The black car stopped trying to move past them but stayed close behind. Then Claire could see movement on the driver's side. "Damn," Dan sighed. He began swerving the car again as he unbuttoned his pea jacket and slipped his right hand behind his back. Behind them, a man was leaning out of the open window and bringing a weapon to bear on them.

"Get down!" Dan commanded. Claire sank lower in the seat, but continued watching the rearview mirror.

Several small popping sounds exploded as Dan swerved, but there was no corresponding sound of bullets striking the car. Dan swerved again as the limo adjusted its position, and the gunman fired several times. Bullets hit the trunk lid with dull thuds.

"Okay, this is it." Dan spoke tersely, his jaw set in anger. "Hold on tight, we're going to go into a spin at this next off-ramp."

"We're what?"

"Just hold on!"

It was only when he lifted his right hand that Claire saw the squat bulk of a gun in it. He lifted his weapon and pointed it back through the shattered rear window, taking crude aim in the rearview mirror.

They were coming up on the off-ramp rapidly, and the road was clear of interfering traffic as the limo moved to put the gunman into position again.

Dan fired four times with a sound like cannon fire in the confines of the car. Claire could see a wisp of steam rise out of the hood of the Lincoln to whip away in the wind. Then the world jerked and spun as Dan hit the brakes and twisted the wheel to the left, throwing her against the door. She had a fleeting glimpse of the black car slipping past on Dan's side as they spun halfway around, and Dan turned the wheel hard the other way as he hit the gas.

They continued their spin partially, then fishtailed the other way, the rear of the car slapping the guardrail of the overpass as they shot ahead of the blue Mustang. Dan hit the brakes again, twisting the wheel, and they rocketed down the off-ramp and skidded in to mingle with the traffic moving through the suburb of Eagan.

"Those guys were downright antisocial," he mumbled, pinballing the car through traffic. "I hope a leak in the radiator will slow them down some. It's almost rush hour. The traffic will hide us."

"You're taking this awfully well." Claire sat up, staring down at the gun on the seat between them.

"Won't do me any good to take it any other way," he said, softly. "We'd better ditch this car and pick up a new one."

"Just leave it?"

"It's rented in my name." He turned off the busy street and approached a quiet residential neighborhood. "I'm sure I'll get the bill when they find it," he said.

Claire sat quietly beside him as he turned through the streets. Her thoughts swirled with images of gunfire and roaring wind and the eerie rush of the world around a spinning car. They finally settled on Dan. Through it

all, this affable man at her side had remained stone
calm. He'd used the gun with familiar ease, like a car-
penter would use a hammer. It was unsettling to see that
side of someone close to her.

Chapter Ten

Dan found a used-car lot in Eagan and ditched their rental on a side street. They walked to the lot and purchased a well-used 1972 Chevrolet Vega, paying just over six hundred dollars for the privilege of sputtering away from the lot in a cloud of blue smoke. But the car served its purpose well: it ran, more or less; it was the cheapest car on the lot; and no one would be looking for them in a clunker of such dubious merits. And though it had trouble running much faster than forty-five, it got them to another luxury hotel.

"I'm afraid we can't return to our hotel, Claire. They must have been following us for quite some time, which would explain how Moss showed up at the right restaurant last night. If they're willing to take potshots at us on a highway, they'll be only to glad to corner us in a hotel room. We'll have to call the hotel and have them gather our things and ship them to your cousin's house in Garner Falls. I'll call the hotel later and make the arrangements."

Claire merely nodded and accepted the warm squeeze of his hand.

"I'm afraid we'll have to eat in tonight, to stay low," he said.

"I'm not in the mood for anything fancy, anyway," Claire admitted. Her voice quavered, and she fought to calm it. "Besides, that's why they invented room service."

"Right you are."

Dan checked them in using an alias card he'd used before, and explained to the porter that they had just left their luggage at another hotel and would be bringing it over soon.

"You order something for us," he told her when they stepped into the double room. "I'm going to shower and call the hotel about our things, telling them an emergency has come up."

Claire looked around the room, her eyes landing on the single king-sized bed. "And just where do you expect to sleep? I don't think there's room to stretch out in that car you bought."

"That's funny, Claire," he said with a tired grin. "But don't worry, we won't be in this room very long. We've got business to take care of tonight."

"Tonight? Haven't we had enough business for one day?"

"Just one little errand, and with any luck we'll be finished." He slipped into the bathroom, but before he closed the door he turned to her. "We've got to break into Harold Jason's house."

Then the door shut before she could utter a single word.

CLAIRE PHONED THE HOSPITAL in Grand Forks while she was waiting for the food to arrive and was rewarded by the first good news she'd heard about her uncle's condition. He'd begun to react to stimuli, and the doctor was confident that he would regain consciousness soon.

She turned on the television, hoping the local news program might have details of what happened in St. Louis Park after they left. The babble of commercials and insubstantial programs was soothing, proving that life was going on as usual and their afternoon ordeal really was just a fluke. She was almost ready to feel optimistic when Dan arrived. Almost, but the day's events clutched at her heart.

Dan's hair was still damp when he entered the room twenty minutes later. He'd showered quickly and gone to the phone to make his call.

"It will be a couple minutes till our food comes," Claire told him after he'd finished. "I called the hospital, and Uncle Walter is starting to come around. I hope we can provide him with a solution to the break-in when he wakes up. More than we've got now, anyway," she added ruefully.

"That's great news about Walter, Claire. And I think we'll manage as best we can."

Claire had bound her cinnamon hair with a banana clip. She sat in a chair by the window and curled her legs up beneath her as she watched him, wondering if their optimism was founded in reality.

She felt a closer affinity to him that afternoon than she could remember ever feeling. Just as Dan's youthful audacity had grown into an adult sureness and reliability, her feelings for him now seemed to come from a deeper well of emotion. Tempered by her own experiences, she felt a greater compassion as she watched him taking his precautions for their safety in the room.

As if sensing the turn her thoughts had taken, he turned from the door and said, lightly, "They really know how to raise them in Minnesota, don't they?"

"What are you talking about?" She returned his consuming stare with a guileless look even as a flush of relief and happiness expanded within her.

"You are without a doubt the most beautiful woman I've ever chanced to meet," he told her. "And you always have been."

"Stop that, Daniel. I think you're trying to confuse me. So much has been happening lately. Don't add to it," she said.

"I don't want to confuse you, Claire." He leaned to touch her cheek with the palm of his hand. "I want you to be very clearheaded about us."

"And what about us?" she replied, softly. The light of the setting sun burned shadows into the minute creases in his face, and Claire's heart shivered as she looked up at him.

"I don't know. Not yet, anyway. Maybe you can tell me."

"I don't know if I understand."

"Will you want me around when we've returned to normal life? I'd like to be, you know. I'd like it very much."

Claire remained silent, letting her growing smile provide its own enigmatic response, and he held her eyes for a long moment. Then, with a sly smile he dipped his head down toward hers.

The first touch of his lips was light, ready to move away if she rebuffed him, but the second kiss was sure and strong, a tender demand for love expressed without reservation. And, when the knock at the door announcing the arrival of their dinner separated them, he moved away slowly, watching her with loving eyes for a long moment before turning toward the door.

"Have you regained your appetite yet?" Dan closed the door behind the departing waiter and approached Claire, standing by the tray.

"Yes, my appetite has improved greatly." Claire uncovered the meal. "I ordered steak. I hope that's to your liking."

"Sounds good to me," he said, watching her, devouring the sight of her. "Everything is very much to my liking."

The six o'clock newscast began just as they finished, and Claire picked at the remainder of her food while listening to the report, her thoughts swirling between the emotion aroused by his kiss and the fear renewed by the newscast.

"We'll have the whole story on that winter storm on the weather later in the newscast," the anchorman was saying as Dan returned to the table. "But first, the news. Our top story tonight concerns the mysterious death of a St. Louis Park man." The newsman began his story about the horror Claire would just as soon forget. But the blank formality of the anchorman's voice helped soothe her nerves, making her part in the discovery seem small and far away, something that happened to someone else.

Video footage of the apartment building replaced the man on the screen as he continued talking. On the TV screen, two attendants were wheeling a stretcher down the walk to their waiting ambulance under the watch-

ful gaze of several police officers standing between the
house and a crowd of onlookers.

The newscaster went on to describe the scene, David
Zendler's background as a security guard at the Walker
Museum, and the fact the police had no leads yet in the
case. Citizens who might have observed something were
encouraged to call a tipster's hot line, and Claire hoped
that no one had observed them snooping around.

"And though they don't know it yet, Garner Falls is
the cornerstone of this tragedy now," Dan said, shaking his head tiredly.

Claire looked deeply troubled. "Dan? Who the hell
is Hans Wermager?"

"Hans and Moss deal in a great variety of stolen high
profit items—Moss doing the stealing and Hans doing
the profiting. He's from East Germany originally where
he was a minor government official who got caught
moving goods across the border for profit. He went
West begging for asylum."

"And they gave asylum to a criminal?"

"Of course. I don't think they knew the full story of
his past, but I doubt it would have stopped them. He
had some information to trade, and they didn't see fit
to turn him down. Unfortunately the freedom on our
side of the wall gave him more opportunity to make
money and keep his operation concealed better. He's a
naturalized English citizen—has been for twenty
years—and his record abroad is clean. It's only here in
the States that anyone has anything on him, and that's
only a flimsy fraud charge that no one has ever pressed
for extradition on. But we have a great deal of evidence
that he's been active in smuggling antiques and historic
documents out of the United States."

"And what were your dealings with him?"

"In Europe, mostly." Dan grinned in apparent amusement. "I met him when I started working for the Customs Department. Hans and I had a business arrangement, you might say, for several years. The last time I saw him was when I rerouted one of his shipments to a New York warehouse. I came back to the States after that."

"This *rerouting* of yours sounds more like a mark against you than him."

"It was a shipment of bootleg Pierre Cardin clothing. Knockoffs headed for sale in the U.S. The crates were being shipped across the Atlantic between two of Wermager's dummy corporations. We couldn't make a case against him, so I pulled a switch at the docks in Marseilles and a load of bathroom fixtures came here instead."

"So that's what you do for a living." Claire laughed at the thought of him hunting down criminals in the fashion industry. It felt good to laugh and to enjoy a conversation. "What happened to the counterfeit dresses?"

"We shredded them." Dan smiled happily. "Of course, Hans believed I sold them myself. He has a small vendetta against me, you could say."

Worry pleated her brow. "It certainly appeared that he held a grudge on the highway this afternoon."

"Mmm," he said, his lips pressed tightly together.

"So where do we stand now? Zendler is dead and your buddy, Hans, is after us."

"I don't know." He made a sour face, his eyes lost in thought. "I had thought that Zendler got what he was after and Hans and Moss carried it away with them after they got rid of Zendler. But if they had the papers, why would they be shooting at us on the highway?''

"They obviously don't have them," Claire stated. "Besides, if Zendler got what he wanted in Walter's shop, why did he bother breaking into two more places?"

"You're right. But if he didn't get it, what happened to the missing crock? What about their method for concealing the documents in a crock. Did your conversation this afternoon help to confirm that hunch?''

"Yes, I think so. The pots Patty Sloan made were cracked on the bottom. He could have cut the flawed base off, made a new bottom for it with the papers hidden inside and made it look like fired clay. There are several types of plastic resins that could be formed cold and left to dry so they wouldn't harm the papers. He probably just coated it with a thin layer of Masonry cement to look real.''

"I'll buy that. But I'd say that we can forget about the crock for now," Dan said. "We'll probably never find it. I'd like to know who Hans is hoping to sell the stuff to when he does get his hands on it. There's an awful lot of money flying around in this deal, so the man on the other end of the pipeline must be a real high roller.''

"He must have had someone in mind to sell it to when he set the theft up.''

"Yes, and it's got to be a pretty die-hard collector to spend this kind of money. If they paid David Zendler twenty-five thousand for his part of the bargain, you can be sure Harold Jason got a fair bundle more than that. And Lord knows how many other people are involved.''

"But if they sell the papers under the table, the buyer can't ever admit having them. Why would anyone spend so much money to get something that he couldn't show off?"

"You'd be surprised," Dan said. "Artwork, for example, is stolen all the time. Most is never seen again, while some pieces have been found in private collections. Some of the people who collect art and historical documents seriously are totally consumed by their need to have certain pieces. It's an addiction with them. I remember an Italian count who had a fair collection of impressionist paintings hidden in a subbasement of his villa. He was the only one who ever looked at them, and they'd probably still be down there if unusually heavy rains hadn't flooded the basement. He had to carry his treasures up to save them from the flood waters, and someone with an eye for art reported him to the authorities. Those paintings were stolen from some of the finest museums on the continent."

"It's hard to imagine wanting anything that badly," Claire mused.

"No, it's not hard at all." Dan carried their dishes back to the room-service cart and returned to sit looking at her earnestly. "Haven't you ever wanted anything so badly that you've felt you might die if you don't get it?"

Claire blushed because she knew what he was suggesting—that he wanted her as badly as ever. This was not the time to surrender to their passion. So she changed the topic. "I've been meaning to ask you—is that package you picked up at the airport a gun?"

"Yes. I've developed the habit of stashing things like that where they might be handy later on. I put the gun there before driving to Winnipeg on the off chance that I would have to fly to the Twin Cities quickly. I knew I couldn't get past airport security with the one locked in my Garner Falls car." He held her hand tightly as he gazed down at the porcelain flesh clasped within his strong fingers. "I didn't want to tell you I had it."

"Why not? Were you afraid I'd object to it?"

"It was partly that, I suppose. And partly the fact that I'm not very happy about carrying it, myself."

"You seemed quite proficient with it this afternoon."

"A diabetic may be good with a syringe, but that doesn't mean he likes it."

"So why do you carry it with you always? And why do you continue doing what you do?"

"I carry it because the people I deal with respect it, that's why. And why do I continue? I don't, actually, not anymore." As he looked at her, the faint glow of streetlights and the twilight sky painting his face blue, Claire saw a look of infinite fatigue and sadness cross his features. For a moment he looked so old, so totally drained of life that she wanted to hold him to her and share what life she could with him. But it was a fleeting image drawn from the light and the serious look in his eyes, and it passed as quickly as it came upon him. "I resigned from the department nearly a month ago," he said.

"You didn't tell me that."

"I hadn't planned on telling you anything at all. When I did, I chose not to include that part of my sordid tale."

"But what about your claim that you needed permission to tell me about your work?" Claire asked. "Wasn't that true?"

"Not permission exactly but, resignation or not, I'm still working for them. You've got to understand how my job for the Justice Department works. There's never been official recognition of my status with the government. I just maintained my cover as a lowlife in Europe and stayed available for assignment while my salary was deposited into an account in the Bank of England. I've helped bust drug manufacturers, smugglers and counterfeiters over the years. And my main effectiveness was that there was never a shred of evidence to connect me to any law enforcement agency. But that's a double-edged sword that leaves me a bit at the mercy of the Justice Department. My resignation is on file, but it hasn't been accepted yet. I'm still on the payroll until my resignation is processed."

"And that's why Burt got those reports? Because the paperwork isn't finished?"

"That's about it. When I finished working for Customs Investigations in Europe, I came back to the country to work for the department of Alcohol, Tobacco and Firearms for the last few years. We were trying to shut down gunrunning on the East Coast. I'd infiltrated one of the main groups and in that position I came under the scrutiny of local law enforcement. I managed to rack up quite an impressive record as a 'known associate' in several police files," he said, laughing. "It's too easy for the bad guys to check up on me, so my police records have to match my story. Some of the reports are simple fiction inserted in the records, while others were the natural result of the position I was in. Fortunately my European record has been corrected in anticipation of my retirement, so he won't find any international warrants out on me."

"That sounds like the perfect job for you, Dan." Claire laughed. "Sneaking and spying. Why did you quit?"

"I loved doing it for a long time. Hell, I was running around Europe playing secret agent and actually doing some good at the same time. But playtime ends and all spies must come in from the cold sometime. It was good while it lasted."

"So why did it end? And, while we're at it, how did you start to begin with?"

He released her hand and leaned back in his chair. "How do I begin a story like that?"

"Why did you leave town, Danny?" she asked abruptly, needing to know now. All the anger and hurt she had stored up over the years needed to be dealt with and cleared away. But he disappointed her.

"I'd prefer to wait with that till later, Claire. It was a mistake that I've regretted many times over, but I feel it would be another mistake to explain it to you right now. I still need proof," he added cryptically.

"Proof?"

"I'll explain it soon. Believe that. Hell, you believed me about my government past. Believe me now when I tell you you'll know soon enough what happened in Garner Falls."

She smiled, surrendering. "You know I didn't need proof of your government background when you wanted me to trust you before."

"I know." He smiled, leaning forward and grasping her hand. "You wouldn't be here with me if you had any doubts."

"And how can you be so sure of that?" Claire grinned, savoring the hands encircling hers. The capacity for violence she'd seen in him earlier was entirely gone, lost in the tender feelings his kiss had shown and his eyes admitted so freely now. And she could feel the corresponding feelings rise within her, washing away any reservations she had. This strong, capable man loved her, and that was suddenly the only thing in the world that mattered.

"I didn't mention that I went to see you once in Vermont." Dan spoke slowly, as if wary of what her reaction might be to his words. "Almost a year ago."

"No, you didn't."

"I went to your antique shop, but you weren't in. I did talk to your partner, though, and I was able to read between the lines somewhat." He looked away then, out the window over the traffic moving on the street as he continued speaking softly. "I don't know why I went there. I didn't know about the divorce, so I guess I was just going to drop in like an old friend passing by. I'd found that it's impossible to just throw away your past and live a new life. You were something good from my past, someone I wanted to keep in touch with."

"Why didn't you find me?" She stroked his hand softly, smoothing away the flexing tension that grew in his fingers as he spoke.

"Because I had thought you were married, you see, and suddenly you weren't. Maybe I didn't trust myself not to act like a fool without the safety of your husband nearby. I suddenly couldn't go through with a re-union, so I sneaked away.''

"You should have come to see me.''

"I know.'' He squeezed her hand firmly. "It was a silly impulse. I won't pretend that I spent all those years dreaming of you, Claire. That would have been rather foolish. But when I got that close to you, I started thinking about how I'd left you before, left everything, and I just didn't feel like facing up to my past.'' Dan lifted her fingers to his lips and kissed them softly, then sat holding her hands as if he was afraid to let them go. "I hope things will be all right soon.''

"I hope so, too,'' Claire said, quietly.

She wasn't sure who initiated the move, but suddenly they were standing by the table locked into each other's arms. His strong arms circled her as he massaged the soft fabric of her sweatshirt across her back. She clutched him with the full urgency of her desire, wanting to feel his lips caressing hers forever.

"I just can't trust myself to be alone with you,'' he whispered.

"It's mutual, Dan.'' Claire pressed her cheek against his broad chest. "I was angry with you back then. You left town and nobody knew why, or at least they wouldn't tell me. And I hated you. Or so I thought. When I saw you less than a week ago, all those hurts, angers, rushed back, surprising me by their force and quietness over the years. I still have trouble coping with them, though I think I have a handle on them now. Yet in the welter of those emotions was also love.''

He looked at her, surprised, earnest. "Claire, we've come full circle you know. Life has brought us back to see if we can do it right this time.''

"Can we?" She lifted her face to gaze into his loving eyes.

"Yes, we can."

She gave in to his lips again, releasing the passion held tightly within her. His strong hands slipped up beneath her top, feeling hot against her flesh. But the touch of his lips and hands were only a teasing glimpse of what she longed for. He still had the power to excite her inner passion after so many years.

And that passion carried them the scant steps to the bed where the taste of Dan's lips and the soft, exploring pressure of his hands were too much for Claire to resist. The need for him, all of him, was too strong for discretion or propriety to hold back.

The years peeled back with the feeling of his wellmuscled flesh beneath her hands. They tore at each other's clothing with desperate need, once more in the grip of the love that had brought them to the first consummation of their relationship in high school. Dan's body, warm and taut with desire, pressed against hers, thrilling her with the soothing motion of his chest over her breasts. His hands massaged down over her back and grasped her hips, drawing her to him as his fingers moved with provocative pressure to the very core of her physical need.

And then he was moving above her, building the electric spark of desire within her to a crescendo even as he tensed as his own needs culminated and he covered her face with kisses.

They'd been swept back into love before they were even aware of where they were headed, carried by the current of emotions that their cautious minds might have put off indefinitely.

"I love you." He sighed and slipped to her side. "And I'm not going to leave you or lose you again. Never again."

"Oh, Dan, why did you go? I need to know now." She had promised not to press, but she felt it was the last wall that stood to keep them separate. "You were the first man I loved, the first I made love to. I thought you loved me, and then you were gone."

"I ran away," he said, squeezing her tightly to him, his heart pounding against her ear. "But it wasn't because I didn't love you."

"But why? Why did you run?"

"Peterson's Hardware was robbed, Claire, and I was the prime suspect. I didn't do it, but Burt let my dad buy me out of it provided I left town. I couldn't have explained it to you."

"I remember the robbery, but I would never have believed you stole the money."

"I know. But you wouldn't have believed my explanation, either. You never believed me about Burt, Claire, not about him."

"What? Do you think he picked you out as a suspect just because he didn't like you?"

"No, he found my penknife in the back room. It was a gift, with my name engraved in the handle, so I can't say he didn't have evidence. All I know is that I didn't lose it back there."

"Who did?"

Dan sighed. "Not now. Let's talk later," he said. "The truth is I don't have any cold hard facts."

"The theft is old news, Dan. How can it spoil things?"

"Please, Claire, don't ask," he implored her.

"It concerns me," she replied evenly. "I deserve an answer."

"Yes, you do," he said. After a long pause he began. "I left town because Walter told me to go. And he warned me not to contact you when I had gone. Walter did! When it came right down to it, he didn't believe me." Dan's arms clenched around her as he spoke. "I'm convinced Burt rigged the evidence and persuaded Walter to his side, then they both went to my father and forced him to make good the money that was stolen. How in hell could I get you believe me with everyone else against me? How could I ask you to oppose your whole family, your whole community?"

"That's why he wouldn't hire you back on the farm? That's why you never contacted me?"

"Yes. He said he didn't want a thief working for him or consorting with you. I loved that man like a father, but he kicked me out. I just couldn't stay."

"Oh, Dan—"

"No." He slid back slightly, looking into her eyes. "I'm not looking for sympathy, Claire," he said resolutely. "I love you, and you love me. I know that as surely as I know my own name. But I don't want anything to throw a shadow on our relationship. I left because they promised that nothing would be said about the robbery if I got out of town. Burt, my father and even Walter, all of them thought I did it. I didn't have the guts to stand up to them and prove my innocence."

"Dan, that was long ago! It was a mistake. It doesn't matter anymore, not to me!" Claire held him tightly, burying her face in his chest. "Maybe Burt didn't like you. Maybe he framed you to get at your father. But this is now, today, Dan. The past can't hurt us."

"You're wrong, Claire," he said, sadly. "Because it isn't the past, and it isn't dead and buried."

"What do you mean by that?"

"Claire—" He sighed, looking very tired and exasperated. "There are things I'm not free yet to tell you completely. I know you've heard this before, but you must believe me, and let me reveal them as I can in my own time. I told you about why I left Garner Falls, as I promised. Do you believe me when I say I'll reveal everything at the right moment, in the right place?"

Claire studied his features, which were earnest and a little sad. She could bide her time a little longer, let him have his final secrets until he felt ready to be fully open with her. She shook her head vociferously. "All right, Dan, I won't pressure you any longer. When you feel you can tell me all that stands between you and Burt, let me know."

He smiled and lifted his hand to graze her cheek. "Thanks."

"All right. We've got work to do tonight, don't we?" She snuggled close against him again, wanting nothing more at that moment than to lie in his arms where she could sleep peacefully.

"Yes, there's always work to do," Dan said, his voice a whisper of regret. "And I hope our work doesn't end badly."

Chapter Eleven

Harold Jason lived in a large Tudor house on a short street paralleling the southwest shore of Mirror Lake in the affluent Minneapolis suburb of Edina. The house was surrounded by a natural barrier of stately pines and muscular oaks that seemed to stand guard over the gabled two-story structure.

Dan drove past the house once, making certain there was no activity at the house. There were no lights visible, but there was a Mercedes sedan parked on the long drive that wound up to the house. Dan parked the car down the street from the house shortly after midnight. They sat for a moment listening to the quiet hiss of a light breeze moving through the trees, waiting, it seemed, for someone to give them the command to move. Dan slipped his hand across to grasp hers, squeezing slightly, and she massaged her thumb over his fingers in gentle response.

"Let's get this over with," he said at last. He tested both of the flashlights they'd purchased at an all-night grocery and handed one to Claire. "I don't really care if we wake Mr. Jason or not, but we'd better be inside and close enough to grab him if we do. Since the shop was closed, the odds are good that he has hit the trail already, but let's take it easy getting in, anyway. Are you ready?''

"As ready as I'll ever be, I guess."

They left the car together, stealing quietly across the broad lawn under the sheltering boughs of the trees until they were against the wall of the house. It had begun to snow as they drove across town, signaling the beginning of what the radio weatherman predicted would be the worst storm in recent years. At this point, however, the fat white flakes that drifted down did nothing more than provide an ironic counterpoint to the severity of their mission.

"How can you expect to find anything in this huge place?" Claire huddled up behind Dan as he crouched to peer through a window. The warmth they shared at the hotel was just a memory now.

"I don't expect anything." He moved swiftly past the window and along the wall to the edge of the building. "But I know for damn sure we won't find anything if we don't look."

"But there will be hundreds of places to hide things in here."

"That's why we didn't wait till later in the night to start looking." He grinned back at her and then walked around the front of the house. They hurried into the shelter of the open-entry porch tucked under an upper-story room and Dan withdrew his leather case of lock picks from his jacket pocket. "We'll do it just like this morning," he said, crouching at the knob of the front door. "Look for places of concealment. I think we can skip looking under furniture, though. This guy will probably favor a built-in safe of some kind."

He twisted the thin wire within the lock and they entered the antique dealer's home quickly, easing the door shut behind them.

Claire switched on her flashlight and moved the beam slowly around the entry hall, keeping it low. A broad staircase of darkly stained wood rose before them, flanked by a passage that led to the rear of the house. On either side of them, double doors led to other rooms.

Dan moved the beam of his own light toward the doors on his right, starting toward them.

Claire followed, and they opened the doors carefully on to what appeared to be a living room. A couch and chairs were arranged in a conversational grouping and a stereo system and television were set inside in a cabinet in a corner.

"Not here," Dan whispered, turning away. Claire closed the doors and followed.

They crossed the entry and opened the other set of double doors. Inside was a room that had to be his office. It was paneled in dark oak with several bookcases with leaded glass doors. A large desk dominated the far side of the room. The leather-upholstered chairs and dark wood gave the room the look of a gentlemen's club from the turn of the century.

They moved their flashlights across the room in concert, the light reflecting from the bookcases. One of the bookcase doors stood open, a tumble of books lying on the floor below the shelves. Dan slashed his light quickly to the desk, illuminating the jumbled papers scattered across the top.

"Damn!" Dan cursed angrily as he strode across to the desk and switched on the brass banker's lamp bowing over the work space. "Someone's been here ahead of us."

Claire joined him at the desk, a thrill of fear climbing up her spine as she moved around to the other side, seeing that the drawers were all open and crumpled papers were littering the floor. On the right-hand side of the desk were a telephone and the slim box of an answering machine. The door to the tape cassette compartment stood open.

"Why would they want the tape of his calls?" she asked, pointing her flashlight at the machine.

"I don't have clue one." Dan collapsed into the desk chair with a sigh. "And I don't imagine there's a clue to be found in this joint now."

"What about a safe?" Claire asked urgently as she looked down at him. "Maybe they didn't find it."

"And maybe they did. Maybe that answering machine tape was our clue. Who knows?"

"You aren't getting discouraged are you?"

"Frustrated. We're chasing our tails on this thing, Claire." He looked up at her, his eyes wide with exasperation. "And just to make things fun, we've got people taking shots at us in the streets."

"I guess we won't find anything if we don't look, so we'd better keep looking," Claire whispered.

He stood, grasping her shoulders in his hands.

"I think you should go back to the car," he said seriously. "There's no guarantee about what we'll find."

"Harold Jason's body, you mean?" she whispered.

"That's a distinct possibility," he said.

"With that in mind, I think we'd better search the house quickly and get out before anyone decides to come back to clean up the loose ends."

"And you have no intention of waiting in the car."

"No intention at all. We're sticking together on this one." She grasped his arm lovingly, assuaging her own trepidation by contact with his solid strength.

"All right then, let's get to it." He turned and switched off the desk lamp, picking up his flashlight and joining her before the desk. "Of course, it's possible that Harold Jason is sleeping peacefully in his room upstairs," he told her. "Whoever went through the office might have found what they wanted and left without waking him."

"And then we could still find our answers."

Driven on by the slim hope of finding the man above in the house, Claire hurried out of the office toward the stairway with Dan in pursuit. They mounted the stairs together, coming up into a hall running the length of the house. A faint light shone through a partially opened door at the end of the hall on their right. They crept slowly along the hall toward the light. It was a distance of perhaps twenty feet but it seemed like twenty miles to Claire when their every step seemed to echo through the silent house.

When they reached the door, Dan motioned for her to wait while he peered cautiously around the frame. He wore a puzzled expression on his face when he looked back at her, then gave a quick thumbs-up and stepped into the doorway. Claire stood closely behind him as he pushed the door farther open, looking through the widening crack between the door and the frame as it opened. She could see the unmoving bulk of a man beneath the covers on a brass bed within the room, a reading lamp glowing dimly on the bedside table.

Dan took a step forward, one hand on the door-knob, and Claire followed with her flashlight held out like a club.

The door suddenly slammed back and knocked them both against the door frame. Then it jerked in and Claire saw a blur of motion as a man jumped forward swinging something in past Dan's upraised hand.

Dan fell back against her, his hands thrust out to fend off the blow as the man struck again, and then he fell to the floor with an agonized groan. The pipe had hit skullbone. Without thought, Claire leaped at the man, swinging the flashlight at the pipe he held in one hand. She struck him twice, on the hand and forearm, and he dropped the pipe. But he stepped away from her next swing and leveled the short barrel of a black revolver at her face.

Claire froze, the plastic shaft of the flashlight grasped uselessly in her upraised hand. It was Moss Hunter, the man she'd seen arguing with Dan in the restaurant the other night.

"Pleased to meet you," he said, without smiling. "Now drop that thing and sit down beside loverboy."

Claire did as he commanded, kneeling to take Dan's head in her lap and push his hair away from his eyes with one hand. He was lying on his back staring up at the ceiling and blinking slowly as he moistened his lips with careful movements of his tongue. A dark bruise was beginning to rise on the left side of his forehead. "Damn," he said at last.

Claire smiled down at him. Tears of relief welled in her eyes, blurring the sight of his feeble smile.

"Touching." Moss leaned to tap the barrel of his gun against Claire's head. "Give me his gun."

"What gun?" she asked, hoping she sounded innocent.

"Play stupid on your own time, girl. Give it to me."

Dan shifted to pull the revolver out from behind his back, staring up at the weapon pointed at Claire's head. Claire took his gun from him and handed it up to the man above her.

"Good, now why don't the two of you move your little hug-and-cuddle act over by the bed."

"Hey, Moss, is this any way to act after such a long time?" Dan rolled to his side and lifted himself slowly on one arm. "How's business?"

"Don't get up, Danny." The man's voice was cruelly triumphant, and he pressed his foot lightly against Dan's shoulder to push him back against Claire. "You wouldn't want me to shoot anybody, would you?"

"No." Dan shook his head slowly, forcing himself to laugh. "But how, exactly, are we supposed to get over to the bed?"

"Crawl, old buddy. Like a sick dog." Moss motioned with his gun, grinning savagely. "Join our antique friend there, won't you? He's not very talkative, but he'll keep you company."

"Come on, Moss, let's be civilized about this. Whatever it is, I'm sure we can come to some sort of understanding." Dan sat looking up at the man as he massaged the back of his head tenderly. "I've got a few bucks stashed away, but I can't get it for you if you do anything rash."

"Move! Now!" The man barked his command, aiming his weapon squarely at Claire's forehead. "I'll pop your girlfriend right now if the two of you don't get a move on!"

"Okay, we're moving." Dan and Claire began crawling across the delicate weave of the oriental carpet on the oak floor. "I see your temper hasn't improved any, has it?"

"Just sit on the floor at the foot of the bed and stop gabbing. Come on now, backs against the footboard."

Claire could hear the man walking then stopping several paces behind them when they reached the bed. Now that she was closer, she could see that the bed-clothes had been hastily pulled over Harold Jason. His bound wrists and part of his face projected from beneath the down comforter. He was breathing, but barely.

They did as Moss said, sitting side by side against the cold brass bars. The wall not six feet away was covered with photographs in a variety of antique frames. It struck Claire as strange that she would notice such things at a time like this, but time seemed to be running in slow motion, every act drawn out by the tension of their situation, much like the events of a car accident must seem to a victim.

"Very good," Moss said. He tossed a short length of coarse rope at Claire. "Now, lady, I'd like you to tie Danny's left wrist to the bedpost. Make a nice knot, because I'm watching."

"What are you going to do?" Claire asked him as she picked up the rope and stared uncertainly into Dan's eyes. "We haven't done anything to you."

"No, you haven't," Moss admitted. "But you will if I let you go. You could still ruin everything."

"Ruin what?" she shot back, glancing his way.

"Shut up and tie his wrist."

Dan nodded his head slowly, giving her strength with his confident expression as he lifted his left hand up to the bedpost. Claire tied him securely but tried to leave as much play in the rope as she could under the criminal's watchful gaze.

"Good," he told her. "Now sit beside him."

Dan grasped Claire's hand with his free hand, squeezing tightly. "You aren't being very fair about this, Moss," he said. "I don't know what you feel I've done to you, but I know for certain that Claire hasn't done anything to harm you. Let her go."

The man approached them then, holding another piece of rope. He'd fashioned a loop in one end and he slapped it at Claire's and Dan's intertwined fingers. "Hold your hand out, Danny," he said. When Dan complied, he slipped the loop over his wrist and pulled it tight. Then he slipped his gun into the waistband of his trousers on Dan's side and passed the rope through the brass bars. He pulled Dan's wrist up tightly against the bar and secured the rope to the bar. Then he grabbed Claire's hand and did the same thing.

"Yeah, I've got reason to complain," he said as he worked. "You stiffed us pretty good in Marseilles, buddy. We were out a fair bundle on that deal."

"But that has nothing to do with your current predicament, Daniel." A new voice cut Moss off. Claire turned her head toward where the voice had come from, but the corner of the bed cut off her vision of the doorway. The precise intonation of the man's voice was familiar from Sunday in the shop when he'd been looking at crockery.

"Hello, Hans." Dan shouted out the greeting as though he was meeting an old friend on a street corner. "What's the deal here?"

"The deal is that you were always interfering with my deals." Hans Wermager walked around to stand before them, watching his assistant finish tying their hands to the center post of the footboard. He regarded them over his hawk nose with gloating excitement and smoothed back the thinning strands of hair over his ear as he spoke. "And, now that it's come to the matter of a certain document, I feel I must do what I can to see that you won't ruin this deal. Or any other deals, for that matter," he said, with a matter-of-fact smile. "It was very accommodating for you to have shown up here tonight. We anticipated your company, of course, but I was beginning to fear you wouldn't arrive before it was time to leave."

"I'm glad we didn't upset your timetable, Hans," Dan said.

"So you aren't here because of Dan at all, are you?" Claire said belligerently. "You were after the crock. You're the one who stole the letter!"

"Claire!" Dan shouted. "Don't—"

"Oh let her talk, Danny," Hans said coldly. "Even if she were so unintelligent as to know nothing about what is going on, we would still kill her along with you. She might as well have her say. Besides, she is quite correct. We want that crock and the oh-so-important letter hidden inside of it."

"Major Holloway's letter," Claire said.

"Exactly, my dear. A great deal of money has already been expended to obtain that letter, and I anticipate an even greater return once I complete delivery of

the shipment. I, myself, have little interest in such things
as old letters, but my client is very anxious to add the
letter to his collection.''

"Why kill anyone, Wermager?" Dan asked.

"Because, having killed that double-crossing traitor
Zendler, we must continue to erase people until there is
no one left who knows of our crimes. It is simple economy. Zendler was just hired help," he continued. "Our
inside man at the exhibition. But it seems that he got
greedy and thought he was smarter than he was. He
tried to steal the crockery containing the letter and upset a very delicate transfer operation in the process. I
would never have had to cross the Canadian border and
risk arrest without his interference, and you two would
have been spared all of this. I don't like being double-
crossed," he added, staring at Dan.

Moss tied Claire's other wrist tightly and then hurried from the room.

"Who am I going to tell?" Dan spoke derisively.
"I'm in no position to go to the police, either."

"But you are, dear boy." Wermager knelt beside him,
grasping his coat with one gloved hand. "After I
learned you were back in Garner Falls, I knew you were
seeking to steal my prize as you did the last time we met,
but my friends overseas told me of the magical trans-
formation that your Interpol records have undergone.
Suddenly you are a very clean citizen, Daniel. In fact,
a certain affiliation you had with your government has
come to light. I understand that you've severed your ties
in that quarter, and they are cleansing your record with
that end in mind. Given your reputation as a Jonah for
so many of your friends, it's a wonder I didn't know
sooner. So, economy dictates that I eradicate you most

of all. I think you should have left things as they were,
dear boy."

"I didn't expect to run into you again, Hans, or I
wouldn't have quit."

"I'm sure you wouldn't have." The man stood, slipping his hands into the pockets of his overcoat. "I'm
sorry there isn't time to discuss old times, friend, but
Moss and I have a flight to catch. We've got to retrieve
our prize."

"You haven't got it yet?" Claire asked, confused.

"No. Mr. Zendler's greed has tangled our operation
up badly. Don't worry, we will set it right."

"Who has it?" Claire demanded. "What happened
to it?"

"No, I think you can die without knowing, dear
girl." Hans smiled, stepping back from the bed and beginning to walk away. "I am not in a talkative mood
tonight, and Moss must be done with his preparations
by now. Goodbye, Daniel," he said, his voice fading as
he walked out of the room. Then he stepped back into
the doorway, smiling. "Such a pretty picture," he said.
"I do regret not being able to stay to watch you burn in
the conflagration we're about to set."

Then he was gone.

"Wait!" Claire shouted frantically. "You can't do
this!"

"Save your breath." Dan spoke calmly, leaning his
head back against the footboard.

"I don't like your friends, Dan," Claire said, struggling to adopt his calm posture as the acrid smell of
gasoline assaulted her. "I thought you had better taste
than that."

"And they seemed like a fun group when I first met them," he said.

"That just shows how wrong first impressions can be." Claire twisted her wrists within her bonds, searching for the angle that would allow her hands to slip free while she fought her growing panic.

"Look at those pictures," Dan said. "Do you see that?"

"Looks like family pictures mostly," she commented. "Except for a couple that must be from college."

"I've got to get a better look at those pictures," Dan said.

"This is an odd time to develop an interest in photography, Dan."

"It's just that, well, I guess it won't matter if we can't get free, will it?"

"No, not really. I'm sure this bed must be antique." The thrill of discovery colored Claire's voice. "And the welds on an old bed may be quite weak." Claire craned her neck to study the metal framework, struggling to maintain her concentration as smoke began to roll into the room along the ceiling. The sounds of fire were audible below them. She twisted her hands around to grasp the upper rail of the footboard, while her feet found a foothold on the lower rail of the bed. Pushing up she held herself in an awkward thrust-forward position. "If it is weak enough, we can bust it apart," she finished.

Claire strained against the old brass even as the ominous crackling sound grew in the hall. There wasn't much time now.

"It's sure worth a try," Dan agreed quickly. He copied her position and they called every muscle into play as the smell of smoke grew more pungent.

The bed creaked slightly, urging them to redouble their efforts. There was another long creak, and then something snapped beneath them and the bed shook, moving the body behind them.

"Bounce on it," he suggested. Smoke was beginning to pour in along the ceiling, and the crackling sound grew louder outside the bedroom door.

They bounced against the old brass, each jolt producing the sound of brittle metal giving way. Suddenly, the bottom rail came loose on Dan's side, dropping away beneath him and sending him sprawling to his knees on the floor.

"Okay," Claire said. "Slip the rope down off the upright."

She moved closer to him, and they pulled the tightly wrapped rope down to where the bar hung free from the lower rail and pulled it off. The rope loosened on Claire's wrist and she shook it off, the circulation returning to her hand in a prickling rush. She turned her attention to the rope binding her other wrist, and, when she finally freed herself, Dan had already closed the bedroom door.

"Good thinking!" he exclaimed, returning from the door.

"What about those pictures?" Claire moved toward the frames on the wall, trying to breathe as shallowly as possible to avoid taking in too much smoke.

"I thought I saw something," he answered. "There's one that looks like a fraternity picture. There, that one." He pointed to a photograph of about twenty college-age boys sitting on the lawn before a brick house. Their clothing and hair length seemed to date the picture from the mid-seventies.

"That's Phillip!" Claire shouted. Yes, it was clearly her cousin with the receding hairline and long side-burns framing a face far too young to be going bald. "Phillip's fraternity picture," she said, grasping his arm in excitement.

"I thought there was too familiar a face!" Dan exclaimed. "This must have been Harold Jason's fraternity, too! He knew Phillip in college. And that's how he knew about the antique shop when he needed a way to get things out of the country. That was what we were missing. Phillip is the connection!" A look of pure disbelief settled on Dan's features as he stared at the picture. "I'd never have picked Phillip."

"No, you can't think he's in on it!" Claire said, appalled by the thought.

"Why not? Would he object to having a few extra bucks in his pocket?" Dan asked hotly.

"But, his own father—"

"Nobody knew Zendler was going to show up and blow the deal. It should have been a harmless scam for him. Blows my grand theories all to hell, but there's the evidence right before us."

"Now it's even more important for us to get back to Garner Falls!" Claire exclaimed.

"Do you think that's where Hans is going?"

"Of course it is! I'll bet Phillip has the crock, and Wermager is betting on that, too."

"Why would you think that?"

"Who else would Uncle Walter have given it to and not written the transaction for it in his book?"

"One of the family."

"Exactly. He wouldn't have it in the receipt book if he gave it away. And he doesn't give items away to just anybody. Only a family member— Oh, no! Then that means that those two animals are going to Phillip's home!"

"We'd better hurry. Let's go and check on Jason."

They rushed back to the bed, pulling the covers away from the still man. He was bound hand and foot and dressed in a pair of slacks and a shirt that had once been white. Now it was stained deep crimson across the chest, and blood had soaked into the sheet below him.

"Oh, no!" Claire gasped, gripping the man's shoulder tenderly, rolling him to his back. "Mr. Jason!" she called. "Harold!"

He blinked once, moving his mouth slowly and emitting a scratching sound.

"He's not going to make it," Dan said quietly from behind her.

"Wait." Claire waved one hand to quiet him as she lowered her ear toward Jason's lips. "He's trying to say something."

"A ock," he said, each word slipping through his barely moving lips in a feeble breath. "Ock." The last word slid out on a rattling sigh, releasing a breath that was not replaced by another. Jason's eyelids lowered shut.

"He's dead." Claire placed her fingers against his throat, praying for some sign of life, but there was no pulse.

Tongues of flame began to lick past the doorjamb, curling around the door and igniting the varnished wood.

"What did he say?"

"He was having a hard time speaking," she said, still staring at the man on the bed. "But it sounded like he said crock."

"That confirms it," Dan said bitterly, moving to the window. "All right, let's get out of here. You first, I can lower you a bit closer to the ground."

Trying to ignore her fear at hanging a story above the ground, Claire climbed out onto the sill and got into position. Dan lowered her down and on the count of three, released his grip of her.

Claire's stomach fluttered as she shot down through the cold air toward the barren bushes below. She slammed into the brittle shrubbery and pitched forward to her hands and knees on the frozen ground. It wasn't a soft landing, but at least she hadn't broken anything.

"Out of the way!" Dan called out above her. Claire stood and moved away from the house.

Dan hung down from the window frame facing the wall. Then he braced his feet against the wall and pushed himself away as he let go. He hit the branches in a half crouch and bounced forward, slapping his hands against the wall.

"Are you all right?" Claire asked, running to him.

"Never better." He emerged from the bushes grinning victoriously.

Claire threw her arms forcefully around him, hugging him to her in relief. "I hope this isn't your normal idea of a good time," she said against his cheek. "I'd never stand the excitement."

"The excitement has just begun." He squeezed her close, spinning her around in the chilly air. "Now we've got to catch an airplane."

They ran across the lawn as the hungry flames lapped over the fine old structure and roared louder and brighter. The fire painted the entire neighborhood in a hellish hue, and Claire and Dan raced across the lawn like ghosts escaping their doomed domain.

THOUGH DAN PUSHED the old car for all the speed it had left in it, they didn't make it to the airport before Northwest Orient flight 809 departed to resume its flight west from New York to Seattle. It would make a short stop in Grand Forks on its way.

The next flight stopping in Grand Forks didn't leave until nine in the morning. They were stopped from running to Phillip's aid by an airline schedule and a few minutes delay in a smoky bedroom, and all they could do was wait in a lounge and try to forewarn Phillip that Hans Wermager was on his way.

Chapter Twelve

"I was beginning to think we'd never get out of the airport," Claire said as the airplane began to taxi onto the runway. She sat watching the thickening snowfall from her window above the right wing of their plane. "I just hope we'll be able to land in Grand Forks once we get there."

It had been a long night. Once they'd found out they would have to wait till morning to catch a flight out, she had tried to call her cousin. But the lines into Garner Falls had been damaged by the storm. And so they'd waited and watched the weather reports on the television and called Garner Falls every fifteen minutes in the airport café while the night passed in growing apprehension.

The leading edge of the storm sweeping in from the Rocky Mountains had hit the northwestern part of the state with heavy rainfall that morning, coating the roads in ice.

"We'll make it, one way or another," Dan said. "And remember that Hans won't exactly be breaking any speed records getting there, either. He's probably sitting in a ditch right now."

"I hope so, we need as many breaks as we can get."
Claire snuggled her head down against his shoulder.

THE PLANE DESCENDED through heavy clouds from the
clear bright sunshine of the upper altitudes into a world
of swirling snow. Turbulence buffeted the airplane,
tensing everyone's knuckles on the arms of their seats,
but the runway was visible through the snow as they
approached. They landed safely.

Claire and Dan wasted no time heading for the door
since they didn't have luggage to contend with. As soon
as they reached the airport, Dan made his way outside
to find the car in the snow-blanketed parking lot, and
Claire tried to phone home once more. The lines were
still down. When she went to the entrance, Dan was
waiting outside, his car unrecognizable beneath the ice
and snow that he'd hastily scraped away from the windows. Claire hurried through the frigid wind to the car,
and they began their journey.

"I'm glad we gassed up before we parked it," Dan
said, squinting past the swirling snow and ice-coated
windshield. "Unfortunately, I don't have snow tires."

"Don't give me any more cheerful news." Claire's
stomach clenched into a knot as she shivered.

They moved slowly along the snow-clogged road between the airport and the interstate highway, spotting
three cars half concealed by snow along the few short
miles. Gusts of wind struck the car with glancing blows,
testing Dan's ability to control the wheel and stay on the
icy road.

"We won't be traveling very fast," Dan warned.

"But your friend, Hans, couldn't have made much
headway, either. And he arrived at night." Claire shiv-

ered within her winter coat, holding one hand over the heater vent to test the emerging air for any sign of warmth. "I hope your heater works, or we'll have pneumonia by the time we get there."

"It'll warm up." Dan's voice betrayed his tension, and his face was set in a determined mask as he squinted through the white blast outside.

They turned onto the highway, bucking against the north wind that hit them head on. The road was slick over most of its surface, except where the wet snow had stuck along the edges and beneath overpasses, and Dan was hard-pressed to hold the car at thirty miles an hour as they drove through the storm with an undulating motion. It took forty-five minutes to reach their turn onto the state highway that would carry them across the river and toward Garner Falls.

Once they left the four-lane highway and headed east, they had to contend with the wind constantly trying to push them off the right side of the road. The flat terrain of the valley worked in their favor by allowing the lion's share of snow to blow unimpeded across the road, but wherever anything rose up enough to hinder the wind, a drift spilled onto the road. It wouldn't be long before the roads were completely impassable.

"We'll never make it over the road to the farm," Claire said. Though the heater had managed to do its job against the frigid weather, she couldn't seem to warm up. It was as if the wind had driven the icy bullets of snow through to the bone, leaving her with a permanent chill. "That's nearly five miles of dirt road."

"The sheriff's department has a four-by-four, don't they?" Dan asked. He glanced at her quickly, trying to smile, but the ordeal of driving through the swirling white mass had taken its toll and his smile was forced. "We'll need four-wheel drive for sure."

"I'm sure they have one." Claire stared out the window, watching the snow billow out in a solid sheet driven on by the fury of the wind. "Watch out!"

Dan jammed the accelerator down hard as the car slammed into a window-high drift that had grown out from a lone tree beside the road. The wheels left the slick pavement as the car slid sideways against the drift and Dan fought to control the wheel. The drift wasn't very wide, and the vehicle forced its way through to the road beyond with a jerk that sent them into a short spin. Dan twisted the wheel into the spin, and the car jumped back until they could continue into the moving wall of white before them.

"If we'd been going any slower we wouldn't have made it through that one," Dan said, relief coloring his voice.

"I don't even know where we are," Claire said. "We're lucky to see a foot of road ahead of the car."

"Don't worry, we'll make it."

"He's had too much head start, Dan. How can we possibly beat him?"

"Don't lose your confidence now, Claire. He's not used to snow, and it will slow him down more than it does us. Remember they didn't reach that nine o'clock plane, either."

They drove on in silence, until Claire could stand it no longer.

"How long have we been driving?" Claire turned away from the window, blinking her weary eyes.

"A couple of hours. We're down to less than ten miles per hour on this road." Dan leaned forward, straining to see. "I think we just passed the Hemming-sen farm, though."

"That would put us about six miles out of town."

"About that."

"Thank God." Claire sank back into the seat, her knotted stomach calming slightly by the thought of stopping safely in town. The journey had been a long slide through the void from one drift to the next, constantly praying they wouldn't be traveling too slowly to pound through the building walls of snow, just as she prayed they wouldn't be traveling so fast that they'd lose control of the vehicle. The calm world of a gentle, hesitant winter they'd left two days before had been transformed into a scene of snarling fury.

"Yes, we're almost there," he said. "Here's Nordstrom's place."

They passed a mailbox, slamming through the snowdrift, and from memory Dan guided the car around the gentle southern turn the road took at that point.

"I used to be able to make it around this turn at sixty miles an hour with my eyes closed," he told her. His smile was tense but relieved.

"We're almost in town." Claire strained forward to see ahead of the car, barely able to discern the edge of the road.

Then the dim outline of a frame house passed on their right, and the wind lessened. The road changed from treacherous ice to a morass of soft snow scraping against the bottom of the car as Dan coaxed them through it. There were houses on both sides now, houses that stopped the wind and forced the snow to clot in the streets.

"I don't think we'll make it all the way downtown, Claire. The snow is too thick and my tires aren't up to it. We can walk any time now that we're in town."

"But not any sooner than we have to, that's for sure. Haven't you ever heard of windchill factors?"

"Don't believe in those newfangled notions, myself," Dan said. "Cold is cold and there's no sense making it sound worse than it is. Still, I'd rather not walk."

Eventually, however, they were forced to abandon the car when the wheels refused to find traction in the soft snow and spun uselessly beneath them. Fortunately they'd made it past the railroad tracks and only had two blocks to walk to the sheriff's office. Huddling up within their coats, they set off through the knee-high snow into the center of the town.

"Don't you people ever shovel your walks?" Dan shouted as they slammed through into the main room of the sheriff's office.

Iris Jordahl, the office clerk, looked up from her typewriter in surprise. She tilted her head to regard them over her half-glasses, then smiled as she recognized Claire.

"Good afternoon, Iris." Claire stamped the snow off her shoes and shook her hair back. "Is the sheriff in?"

"Not at the moment. Don't tell me you've been walking in this weather." Iris skewered Claire with a look of motherly concern.

"Yes, and it's a vicious day for walking," Claire told her. "I have to use your phone."

"You can try it. But the lines have been down all night and morning."

Claire dialed Phillip's number once more, tapping one thumb nervously on the counter as she waited. "Still out." She dropped the receiver in place, scowling.

"I thought so. We've been going through hell here since yesterday afternoon. First the power went and then the telephones, and now Burt is out there somewhere helping Charlie Tollefson out of a ditch. Grown man like Charlie should know better than to go out on a day like this, but then Lord knows there's more than enough fools out there in the storm right now." The gray-haired woman raised an eyebrow on the last comment, watching Dan and Claire shake the snow from their coats and stamp their feet on the rug inside the door.

"What about the deputies?" Dan said, approaching the counter between them and the plump woman. "Who's available right now?"

"Jimmy should be back in a couple of minutes. He just radioed in a minute or two ago to say he was on his way. Why? Is there something wrong, Daniel?"

"We don't know, Iris." Dan leaned on the counter, water dripping onto the polished surface.

"Where is Jimmy?" Claire asked Iris.

"That old elm by Violet Truedson's gave way and broke in her kitchen window. He went to help board it up. She just papered the walls in there before Thanksgiving, too. I hope it wasn't ruined."

"Does he have a four-wheel drive vehicle?" Dan asked, cutting off the woman.

"He's got the Jeep."

"Good."

"Do you think we're too late?" Claire's voice was tight with anxiety when she spoke, and she moved to the other side of the counter and took Dan's hand.

"I have no idea. Wermager may not know where the farm is. For that matter, he might not have made it to town yet." Dan squeezed her hand tightly in his, offering his own self-assurance as a balm to her nerves. "We need a good vehicle to get out there and see for ourselves."

"Just as long as you aren't planning on stealing a vehicle." A man's voice came from the holding cells area behind the counter, and Dan and Claire turned to see Jimmy Webster come in, slapping snow from his down-filled winter jacket. "You two picked a hell of a day to come back," he said.

"We need some help, Webster," Dan said.

The deputy walked around the desk holding his cold gaze on Dan's face. He didn't say anything until he was standing directly before him.

"You're still a smartass, aren't you, Garner," he said. "You could have stopped the game anytime by telling Burt who to call for the real story, but you just wouldn't do that."

"What are you talking about?" Dan asked.

"Your agency clearance came down the line yesterday morning." Jimmy slapped his uniform cap against his leg and laid it aside on the countertop. "Okay, what did you two find out that brought you flying back here in the worst damn weather around anyone can remember?"

"I'm sure you heard of the theft in Minneapolis last month, haven't you, Jimmy?" Claire spoke excitedly, grasping his forearm. "The Holloway letter?"

"Of course. It's on the news every five minutes. Somebody took a bunch of old papers and the world got excited about it. Why?"

"That's what they wanted in the shop!" she said. "They used Walter's antique store to smuggle things out of the country, but someone got greedy and tried to get it away from them."

"Is this getting back to that crockery garbage again?"

"Come on, Jimmy," Dan said. "If you can believe I'm a cop, you can believe anything, can't you?"

"I only believe what can be proved with physical evidence," he said. "You'd better fill me in. Come on, we'll use Burt's office."

"There's no time for talk. There's a couple of men on their way to Phillip's farm to get the stolen goods as we speak."

"I saw Frank Tillson talking to a couple of guys in a Scout around noon," Jimmy said. "He said they'd asked the way to Phillip's place."

"My God, that was them!" Claire cried out. "We're too late!"

Dan took her hand. "Come on, Jimmy, let's move."

"Okay, I've got reason to believe you. We'd better move fast." Jimmy took his revolver out of its holster. "The storm is beginning to play itself out, but we're almost out of daylight, and I'm not real hot on trying to find the farm in the dark." He flipped open the cylinder and spun it once, then snapped it shut with a flick of his hand. "You armed, Danny?"

"I've got a .38 in the car."

"Better take one of our shotguns, too," Jimmy said.

"This is great," Dan said as he and Claire followed Jimmy out to the gun cabinet. "I'll make a lot of friends fast if I start blasting holes in their interior decorating with a scattergun."

"It's a little late in life to start worrying about making friends, Garner," Jimmy said, handing him a short-barreled pump shotgun. "I assume you know how to use one of these."

"I'd say so."

"Good. Now, Claire, I'd like you to fill Burt in when he gets here," the deputy said, zipping his coat shut. "He'll have to take steps to surround the farm as soon as the storm lets up."

"I'll leave him a note," she said, putting on her gloves.

"Please, Claire, I think it would be best if—"

"Save your breath, Deputy," Dan cut the other man off. "There's no time to waste on an argument that you'll lose anyway." He took Claire's hand as they headed for the door.

IT WAS NEARLY FULL DARKNESS when they reached the gravel road leading out to the farm. Though the fury of the storm seemed to have abated, snow swirled around to keep visibility low. The road itself was barely visible and Jimmy had to drive very slowly to keep them centered between the snow-filled ditches that would swallow their vehicle on either side of the narrow track.

The wind screamed around them as they picked their way through the featureless white world. Claire huddled against Dan in the front seat with the deputy straining forward as they drove. Finally, after spending nearly an hour covering the twelve miles between town and the farm, they could make out glow of the yard light and the mailbox with Hoffner spelled out in black lettering on the side.

Jimmy found the driveway into the farmyard and turned in carefully. Parked against the hedge separating the front yard of the house from the drive was a Scout four-wheel drive vehicle—the same car whose occupants had been asking directions earlier in the day.

Claire felt raw fear well up inside her as she realized that the moment of truth had come.

Chapter Thirteen

"I'll go up and knock on the door." Jimmy leaned slightly to talk to Claire and Dan squeezed in beside him. "I'll say I got lost in the storm and I'm looking for someplace to wait it out."

"How can we get in?" Dan asked Jimmy. Claire was sitting in the center of the seat and Dan slipped his arm around her shoulder as he looked across at the officer. "Hans will certainly have Moss check for any extra people sneaking around outside after Jimmy goes in."

"The cellar door!" Claire said, turning her head from one man to the other. "They've got an old cellar door on the north side of the house. I'm pretty sure they put in a new door at the base of the steps inside, but at least we can get in out of the storm while you use your pick on the lock."

"Doesn't Phillip lock the outside door?" Dan asked her.

"Not the outer one," Claire said. "At least, he never has."

"Good." Jimmy spoke with confident authority. "I'll make sure there's no keys in that Scout, and then head up to the door."

"Then what?" Claire asked. "How will we know what to do?"

"Sneak up the basement steps and listen at the door to the kitchen." Jimmy regarded the hedge and the gray void beyond it where the farmhouse was totally obscured by the swirling snow. "I'll see if I can't get out to the kitchen at some point. Wait, when they put in the new furnace, did they leave the old heat vents in?"

"I think they must have." Claire thought hard to remember the fate of the old ornate floor grates. "I'm sure they did in the upper rooms, anyway, but I don't know about the main floor. The basement has been remodeled, you know."

"If any of the old ductwork is still in place, you should be able to hear quite a bit of what's going on through that," Jimmy said. "Just keep your ears open and be ready to move."

"Don't you do anything stupid, Webster," Dan cautioned. "Claire and I aren't exactly a SWAT team, you know."

"I'll keep that in mind." The deputy laughed. "Let's get a move on now."

"Good luck, Jim." Claire kissed his cheek lightly, then pulled her stocking cap down snugly over her ears and turned up the collar of her coat. "Let's go."

Dan forced the door of the car open against the wind and jumped out holding the shotgun close to his chest. Claire emerged into the tearing blast of the wind, turning her back to it as Dan let the door slam shut in the wind. She put her arm around Dan's broad back and they trudged through the snow together looking for the sidewalk.

Once they'd found it Dan tipped his head toward hers and shouted, "We'd better try to stay far enough from the house to avoid anyone seeing our footprints."

"Okay. We'll have to walk into the wind for about thirty feet or so, and then turn left," Claire shouted back. The wind drove needles of ice into her face and stole her breath away as they leaned into the wind and stumbled north.

After continuing for several torturous steps along a hedge, they turned left and walked into the void. There was nothing to guide their path but the diminishing glow of the yard light through the gray swirl of snow to their left. Snow blasted into Claire's ear where the stocking cap had been pulled up, and she tugged the cap firmly into place while hugging Dan closer to her.

"How far?" he shouted. Snow stung their eyes and packed in along their collars, sending icy fingers down their backs. Their legs moved like wooden stumps, knees stiff and feet numb in the all-too-thin protection of their jeans and shoes.

"I don't know! Just keep walking!"

The yard light began to fade as they continued, and they curved around, continuing on what they hoped was a diagonal path from their original track. But the light faded and then stopped entirely, leaving them in the black hell of winter's icy breath.

"I don't know where we are, Dan!" Claire fought the panic out of her voice as she struggled to find some sense of direction in the spinning blackness.

"Stand still!" he shouted. "We should have been going pretty much due west when the light went out! Try to turn exactly ninety degrees to the left again and walk straight ahead. I think the light was cut off by the house!"

That made sense, and Claire turned with him and began walking cautiously forward. With nothing to guide them, each step felt like stepping off the edge of a cliff in a black tunnel.

Suddenly, Dan stumbled and dropped to his knees beside her.

"Damn!" he shouted, his angry voice barely discernible against the howling storm.

"What happened?" She knelt beside him, her knees sinking into the icy drift of snow.

"We must have found the house! I believe I just tripped against the old cistern!"

Claire groped her frozen fingers into the snow beneath her fallen partner, touching the wooden frame of the old water tank buried beneath the north yard of the house. A sudden memory of being chased away from the dangerous old pit by her aunt on a summer day so long ago brought a brief flash of inspiration to her mind.

"Straight ahead!" she called. "Five feet at the most! The cellar door should be almost straight ahead!"

They staggered to their feet and moved forward eagerly with outstretched arms until the faint light coming through a window grew ahead of them and helped them see the new aluminum siding on the house. The cellar door wasn't more than two feet to their right, and Dan groped for the hasp.

"There's a lock on it!" he shouted.

"What?"

"No, wait a second. It isn't snapped shut. Hold this."

He handed her the shotgun and bent to fight open
one of the heavily snow-laden double doors. A second
later, he ushered her down the steps and eased the
slanted door shut.

The wind rattled behind them, as if angry at being
abandoned.

Claire put the shotgun down carefully and shook the
snow from her coat as Dan flashed his light around the
small space they were crouched in together. The light
reflected around the dusty cement enclosure and Dan's
face looked like something chiseled out of rough stone
in the dim light. He struggled to remove one glove and
flexed his fingers slowly, painfully. Then he unbuttoned his pea jacket and shook the snow out of it, every
movement reflecting the painful cold they'd escaped.
He tried the doorknob, finding it locked.

"Hold the light on the knob, won't you?" he said,
taking the case from his inner pocket and removing a
lock pick.

She took the flashlight and directed the beam at the
knob of the steel door Phillip had installed a couple of
years earlier. The old cellar door had been too drafty,
adequate for an old farm basement of stone and dirt,
but not up to the task of keeping the elements out of the
newly remodeled family room and storage rooms they'd
built into the new foundation. The only reason he'd
kept the cellar door at all was to provide an emergency
exit in case of fire. Now Claire crouched on the cracked
old concrete steps and watched Dan maneuver the slim
wire into the lock with awkwardly stiff fingers.

"Jimmy must be inside by now," he whispered as he
concentrated on his task with the lock. After a couple

of moments of fumbling, the knob turned and the door gave with a soft creaking sound.

Taking the gun in hand, Dan pressed against the door, gritting his teeth as it squeaked open with what seemed like earthshaking volume. Cold air whistled in past them, fighting the warmth of the basement. They slipped through the door and shut it behind them before they'd started a noticeable draft.

They'd come in through the furnace room, which took up one corner of the basement. Claire found the chain switch for the light hanging in the middle of the unfinished room and clicked it on. It remained a dark, brooding place despite the renovations and the addition of a new furnace. Where the old furnace had sat in a corner of the room, several steel ducts hung unattached near the floor joists exposed in the ceiling. Dan walked over to stand beneath them, listening intently.

"Anything?" Claire joined him, speaking quietly.

He raised one finger to his lips, cocking his head beneath the open pipe. Voices drifted down faintly, a woman speaking.

"Sit over by the fire, Jimmy," she was saying. "We're opening an inn for stranded travelers." Claire could hear Janet Hoffner's distinct laugh echo through the old ductwork, and a man responded with something she couldn't make out.

"You two picked one hell of a day to visit the north country," Jimmy said loudly. "That your Scout outside?"

"Yes, a rental." They could recognize the clear diction of Hans Wermager's voice above them in the living room of the house, but the rest of what he said was muffled by new flooring and carpet laid over the old ducts on the first floor.

"I got turned around in the storm," Jimmy said, replying to an unheard question. "Had to help pull a car out of the ditch and went the wrong way home like a damn fool. A fella should really have a compass on the dash of his car."

"I always said our sheriff's department couldn't tell one direction from another on a good day." A third man spoke up in amusement—it was Phillip.

"There's four of them." Dan led her back from the duct and whispered into her ear. "Where do you suppose the kids are?"

"Glued to a television set somewhere, I'd imagine," Claire said. "What about Moss? I haven't heard him yet."

"You won't—not with his master present." Dan grinned crookedly, the mocking light she'd seen in his eyes on the highway the other day returning. "He's strictly a 'speak-when-spoken-to' type of underling."

"Then we can't be sure where he is unless Jimmy says something."

"He'd better not say much more," Dan told her, walking slowly toward the furnace-room door. "He must be bellowing like a bull moose up there to be heard so clearly. Hans will get suspicious."

"Let's get into position," Claire said. She grasped the doorknob and turned it slowly.

The room beyond was dimly lit by a floor lamp standing within an arrangement of couches and chairs grouped near the television at one end. The television was off, but the face of the stereo amplifier glowed with green light and the cord of a headset trailed down from the front panel to disappear over the back of the old overstuffed couch. Claire tapped Dan on the shoulder, nodding toward the couch she'd slept on earlier that week, and they crept over toward the light.

A young girl was lying on her side with the slim headphones clamped over head as she read a paper-back book. Claire slipped around the couch and knelt beside her.

"Aunt Claire!" Elizabeth Hoffner pushed herself up, startled, and Dan's broad hand clamped over her mouth before she could say any more.

"Quiet," Claire whispered, holding a finger to her lips. "Don't make any noise. Okay?"

The girl nodded her head quickly, curiosity replacing the brief flash of fear that had filled her eyes when Dan grabbed her. He released her now, and she sat up, removing the headset.

"What's going on?" she whispered.

"How long have those two men been here?" Claire asked.

"Them? A couple of hours, I guess. They'll probably be stuck here all night. Gross, huh?"

"It's more than gross, honey," Claire said. Dan came around the couch to join her, crouching before the slim girl, and Elizabeth's eyes widened at the sight of the weapon he held in his hand. "Those guys are criminals, Lizzy. We've got to get them before they do anything to you or your folks. Where is Paul?"

"In his room. He's got the flu and Mom sent him up to rest with the vaporizer. Are they really crooks? What did they do?"

"They're looking for something and they think it might be hidden here in the house."

"Here?"

"Did your daddy bring home a crock from Grandpa's store?" Dan asked.

"Yes, I think so. That was a few weeks ago. Why?"

"We think the bad guys hid something in it. That's what they're after."

"That's stupid," the girl scoffed. "It's just a dumb old pot."

"Where is it?" Claire asked urgently. She began removing her winterwear as she spoke.

"In the living room. Dad uses it to keep kindling for the fire."

"Great, everything is in one room," Dan said.

"Who is this guy, Claire?" Elizabeth regarded Dan with a mixture of interest and disdain.

"This is Dan Garner. He's an old friend of your dad's and mine."

"I've heard about you." And her tone indicated that what she'd heard probably hadn't been good.

"I'm sure you have." Dan smiled. He removed his coat and cap, dropping them on the floor before the couch. "We're going to go upstairs now. Deputy Webster is already up there in the living room with them."

"Jimmy? How come they just let him in? I mean, if they're such desperate criminals, they wouldn't want the law visiting would they?"

"They're just playing it cool until the storm dies down. They can't go anywhere as long as the roads are impassable and visibility so low," Claire explained. "Then they'll take the crock and run."

"And that's the part we're worried about," Dan added. "We've got to catch them off guard before they have a chance to go through with whatever they've got planned.''

"What do you want me to do?" the girl asked, eagerly slipping forward on the couch.

"Nothing. You sit tight down here so we don't have to worry about you."

"I could create a diversion," she suggested.

"You'd just be a target, Elizabeth. Please stay down here where you're safe." Dan spoke with tender finality, and the girl fell silent. "Let's go, Claire."

Claire patted her niece's cheek and then stood. "Everything will be all right, honey."

They mounted the steps to the next floor slowly, being careful not to make any more noise than absolutely necessary. They paused at the door at the head of the stairs.

"Open the door slowly," Dan instructed. He stood on the landing with his back against the door as he held his weapon ready.

He crouched slightly as she reached past him to turn the knob and push the door. It swung open silently, and he moved through in a crouch with the barrel of the gun covering the kitchen as he turned right to peer through to the dining room. After an anxious moment, he nodded and Claire joined him in the room.

Wind rattled the windows across from them, and a chill draft seeped past their ankles.

The smell of baking ham filled the kitchen, and pans of vegetables and potatoes simmered on the stove. They closed the basement door silently, standing against the wall beside it. Claire found herself looking up at the homey sight of the antique teapots Janet kept high on a shelf along the entrance from the dining room. It seemed so strange to be standing there in the familiar kitchen listening for the sounds of the killers in the living room.

"I am in sales," Hans was saying. "My friend and I were hoping to begin distribution of our dinnerware line in your area."

"What, door-to-door?" Phillip spoke casually.

"No, through retail stores, of course." Wermager laughed heartily.

"I'm going to check on dinner." Dan tensed as Janet's voice shot through to them from the living room and the small creaking of her footsteps on the oak floors approached. "I'll be just a minute."

She stepped through toward the stove and Dan grabbed her mouth as he had done to Elizabeth while Claire rushed to let the woman see her and grabbed her flailing arms. Janet froze when she saw Claire, questioning with her eyes.

"Quiet," Claire whispered. "Okay?"

Janet nodded and Dan released her mouth. She turned to regard him with confusion growing in her eyes.

"Good to see you, Janet," Dan whispered. "No time to talk now. We came with Jimmy to arrest your houseguests. I'd like you to go downstairs and wait till we come for you."

"But I've got dinner."

"Turn off the burners and it will keep just fine," Claire advised her. "Is Paul still upstairs?"

"Yes. What's going on?" she whispered as she turned off the burners under the simmering pots.

"They want the crock Phil brought home from the shop."

"Please go downstairs." Dan steered her toward the basement door. "We've got to hurry."

"Janet?" Phillip called out from the other room. "Honey?"

"Wait a second." Dan stopped her at the open door. "Answer him. Call him in here."

"Yes, Phillip?" Janet said, somewhat timidly. Dan flattened himself against the wall by the door, waiting.

"How's it coming?"

"Fine. Could you come out here?" Janet's voice cracked slightly.

"Just a second."

"I could help, Mrs. Hoffner." It was Hans Werma-ger replying now. "I'm not without talent in the kitchen."

"No," Janet answered quickly. "That's all right."

"Oh, hell." Dan grimaced in exasperation, and prompted Janet toward the basement door, closing it quietly behind her. Then, with a quick nod to Claire, he spun around the corner and walked quickly through.

Claire hesitated a second, then hurried behind him.

The kitchen opened on to the dining room through a hall of about six feet. On the left twin glass-paneled doors opened to living room. Dan aimed the gun through the opened doors at waist height and approached.

Claire could see Jimmy Webster sitting on a chair near the front window across from the door. He stood when he saw Daniel approach, and that's when Claire saw the other man seated on the couch beside him. Jimmy's movement alerted Moss Hunter, and he turned to look directly at Dan and Claire, alarm twisting his features.

"Hold it!" Dan shouted as Moss jumped up and to the side, pulling a revolver from beneath his jacket.

Jimmy kicked out at Moss's legs as he drew his own gun, sending the smaller man sprawling, and the room burst into a sudden storm of movement. Hans and Phillip were rising from the couch on the right, the East German reaching out to wrench the surprised farmer's arm up behind his back as he kicked the coffee table away. He pulled a switchblade from his coat pocket and clicked it open. Then he pushed Phillip into Dan, staggering him back off balance and ran toward Claire at the door.

In the same instant a shot rang out, and Jimmy collapsed and knelt behind his chair holding his arm. He tried to lift his revolver, but it fell from his quivering fingers. Moss was standing then, moving like a cat for a second shot, and Dan pushed Phillip away as Claire struck out at the tall German.

"No!" Dan shouted, rushing the gunman. He swung the shotgun at Moss's gun and kicked down on the man's left knee as the two weapons connected. Another shot rang out as Moss cried in pain, and Dan swung the butt of his weapon up into the man's jaw with enough force to flip him onto his back. Moss lay still on the floor.

But Hans had caught Claire's arm and twisted it up behind her back as he pulled her to him with one hand holding the knife under her chin. "Drop the gun!" he shouted as Dan brought the weapon up to bear on him.

Dan stared at him for a moment, then dropped the gun.

"I want the crockery, Garner," Wermager said, breaking the palpable silence that had descended on the room.

"Go and get it." Dan glanced over to the fireplace where the crock sat with kindling wood standing up in it.

"Bring it."

Wermager motioned the knife slightly away from Claire's throat, and she grabbed his arm with her free hand and slammed the heel of her shoe down on the arch of his right foot. Then she twisted in his grasp, reaching back to claw at his face with her fingernails even as Dan retrieved his gun and rushed the man holding her. Hans pushed her away toward Dan, slowing him slightly as they collided and the gun dropped to the floor. But Dan sprang to his feet before Hans could escape and grabbed him, spinning him and ducking as Hans's blade flashed overhead.

Without hesitation Claire snatched the gun from the floor and rose to jab it forward, aiming at the side of Wermager's head as he prepared to slash the knife at Dan again. "Stop it!" she shouted, the steel of determination in her voice.

Hans jerked back with an angry snarl, but the momentum of the fight had shifted, and Dan caught his wrist and twisted the deadly blade down and away until the East German resigned himself to his fate. The knife clattered to the floor.

"You are lucky to have the woman to do your thinking, Garner," the German spat disdainfully.

"Damn right I am," Dan agreed. "More than you could ever know."

They had no sooner disarmed Hans than a deep voice called out from the kitchen, "So, you work for the government!"

Claire spun to point the gun at the newcomer. Burt Peterson walked in holding his own revolver loosely at his side.

"Don't shoot me, Claire," he said with a laugh. "I'm on your side."

"Uncle Burt, you shouldn't sneak up on people like that." She lowered the gun and accepted the lawman's gentle hug.

"Justice Department," he said, eyeing Dan curiously. "Well, I always said they were crazy in Washington."

"I wouldn't argue with you on that, Burt," Dan said.

"You wouldn't, would you? Another minor miracle. Well, you may be some kind of fancy government agent, but this is still my county, so I'll take this turkey off your hands."

"Go right ahead." Dan took his gun from Claire and stepped back from Hans, who stood calmly appraising them as they spoke. "You'd better get your family, Phillip."

"Hit the deck, Wermager," Burt commanded, taking his handcuffs from the pocket of his parka. "Iris said you headed out here, Claire. Thought maybe I'd crash your party." He knelt to snap the cuffs onto the suddenly cooperative prisoner as he spoke. "Got here too late for the fun, though."

"Better late than never," Claire said happily. "But how did you get here through the storm?"

"The storm is moving south. Dying fast." Burt stood slowly, lifting Hans to his feet by the chain of the cuffs. "You can see starlight out there now."

"We've got a wounded prisoner in here," Jim called out from the living room. "And I managed to take a hit, too."

"Then I'd better get the bunch of you into town." Burt dragged Hans to the living room to inspect the damage. "How's it feel, Jimmy? Damn! Who rearranged this other fella's kisser?"

"Guilty," Dan said as he and Claire followed the lawman in to stand over Moss Hunter, who was just beginning to regain painful consciousness.

"Good work, Garner." The sheriff looked at Dan with a kind of grudging respect then, shaking his head. "Let's get his coat on him," he said. "Gotta get these men to a doctor."

"What about the crock?" Claire asked, moving toward the fireplace.

"Never mind that now," Burt said. "Find his coat and help me get him out to my vehicle. You and Garner can bring in the booty when you come."

Claire did as she was told, and Janet and Elizabeth came up warily to lend a hand. Dan stood guard over Hans, who watched them in apparent amusement as they worked to bundle up his groggy henchman. Then they carried him out to the sheriff's vehicle parked beside the others.

The storm had broken quickly, its wind slowing, the snow ceasing to fall, leaving only loose snow to stream along the ground like an ocean current. If they had arrived half an hour later, Wermager would surely have gone ahead with his plans, and the possible consequences lay colder in Claire's mind than the icy wind that stung her face. She took comfort from Dan's arm as they returned to the family waiting in the farmhouse.

"I was right about that stupid crock," Phillip was saying angrily as they joined them. "That damn Harry Jason put my family in danger for some old paper. I hope they throw away the key when they get him behind bars."

"He can't be arrested now, Phil," Claire said. "Your houseguests killed him before coming here."

"Killed him." A look of shock passed over Phillip's features. "Damn."

"And they could have done the same to us," Janet said, her face paling along with her husband's.

"But it's all over now," Dan said. "Why don't you bust that crock open and give us a look at what the fuss was all about while I talk to Phil about something." He gave Claire a significant look as he spoke. "Could we have a word in private, Phil?" he said, touching the farmer's arm lightly.

"Sure." Phillip shrugged and led Dan toward the small office just off the living room.

"Dan? Can't it wait?" Something was still wrong, and Claire called out to stop the accusations that Dan was sure to level against her cousin once they were alone.

"No." He looked back at her with hopeless resignation in his eyes. Though the duty pained him, he was determined to complete his assignment and question Phillip about his connection to the dead antique dealer. "I won't be long."

"What's that all about?" Janet watched them in curiosity.

"Nothing," Claire said absently. "Where's Lizzy?"

"Upstairs waking her brother." Janet smiled. "He's going to be upset about sleeping through all this mess."

"Yes, I suppose so," Claire said slowly, then she shook her head in annoyance with the thought that refused to crystallize in her head. Something was still wrong. "Come on, let's take a look at what's inside this pottery."

"JUST WHAT ARE YOU accusing me of?" Phillip Hoffner stood beside his desk in the farm office, straining to keep his voice down as he glared at Dan standing uncomfortably before him.

"I don't know, exactly," Dan said. "That's why I'm asking."

"Well, sure, I was in the same fraternity as Harold Jason down at the university," he answered. "A lot of people were."

"Yes, but you're the only one whose dad runs an antique store near the Canadian border. Someone had to set up the transactions. Walter wouldn't have swallowed some lame story about why Jason wanted to sell his stuff so cheaply unless someone close to him broached the subject first. You knew Jason, and you needed extra cash. Come on, Phil, you had no way of knowing what would happen to Walter. Nobody's accusing you of that."

"I'm about ready to knock your teeth down your throat, Danny." Phillip slammed his fist on the desktop, stepping forward. "Do you really think I'd use my old man like that?"

"Nothing would make me happier than to be proven wrong," Dan declared.

"I don't have to prove anything!" Phillip shouted.

"How did Hans know to come here?" Dan shot back. "You aren't listed in the receipt book. There's no way he would have known about the crock being here unless you were in on it all along!"

"Okay, I figured some of it out after I talked to Claire the other day." Phillip spoke more calmly, the cords of his neck taut with the effort to keep from shouting. "I never knew who Dad was buying from in Minneapolis. It isn't my shop, and I never much cared where he got that junk. But then Claire mentioned some guy in the books named Jason and said how the thief was looking for a Redwing crock. I got a two-gallon crock from Dad. I didn't make the connection right away, but after I thought about it, I figured it must be Harry. I told him about the place when we were in college together as students. So I phoned him. He didn't act impressed during our brief conversation. He said he'd get back to me later. Then the storm hit, and the lines went down."

Dan paused, a perplexed smile coming to his lips. "And he dropped your name when Hans and his friend were torturing him!"

"Oh damn!" Phillip muttered, upset.

"But why did you have the crock to begin with?"

"We wanted something for kindling. Walter didn't think the pot was any good. Go look at the damn thing, it's all scratched up. He didn't figure it would sell, so he gave it to me. He tossed it in on the deal when I bought the clock for Janet. That's what I told Jason on the phone, and that's all there is to it, Dan. Dad probably didn't mark it in his book because I didn't pay him anything for it.''

"But, if you didn't introduce Jason to your dad, who—''

"Dan!'' Claire burst into the room flushed with excitement. "This isn't it!'' she cried out. "It's empty! We broke the crock open and there was nothing in it!''

Chapter Fourteen

"Wermager is locked up in the county jail, and Moss Hunter is in the hospital." Dan spoke tiredly into the telephone, sitting on the edge of the bed in his motel room.

"And the crock was empty?" The voice on the other end of the line was tense, angry.

"Yup, just an ordinary old piece of crockery. So we've got our smugglers, but no letter. And I was wrong about our local connection."

"It wasn't the sheriff?"

"No. Jason went to college with Phillip Hoffner. He found out about the shop there, and must have remembered about it when he started his smuggling operation last year. We won't know how it was set up till Walter comes out of the coma."

"If he comes out of it."

"Oh, shut up," Dan said angrily. "Dammit, Peters, I was so sure it was Burt! After all the crap he was pulling off when I was in school here, I figured it had to be him. But I can't find any solid connection. There's no way he could have known Harold Jason."